The Neon Jacket

The Neon Jacket

by Paula Handler

Kids Can Press Ltd.,
Toronto

Kids Can Press Ltd. acknowledges with appreciation the assistance of the Canada Council and the Ontario Arts Council in the production of this book.

Canadian Cataloguing in Publication Data

Handler, Paula
    The neon jacket

ISBN 0-921103-67-0

I. Title.

PZ7.H35Ne 1989 j813'.54 C89-094341-9

Printed and bound in Canada by Webcom Ltd.
Edited by Charis Wahl
Typeset by Pixel Graphics Inc.
Cover design by N.R. Jackson

89 0 9 8 7 6 5 4 3 2 1
The Neon Jacket

For Edward

CHAPTER ONE

I WAS FREEZING. Wet snow kept melting on my lashes. Four blocks to the subway.

"Annabelle! Annabelle Lang. Wait, please!"

I turned. A blast of cold air swept my face. Mrs. Wexler was running toward me.

"Did you not hear me, Annabelle?" she panted, coming up alongside, her big boobs heaving.

"No, Mrs. Wexler, I'm sorry," I shouted over the blaring horns, my teeth chattering.

I was surprised she knew my name. She teaches English to the senior school. I'm the lowest of the low.

"Would you mind delivering this to Bernice Maxstead? I know you both live downtown."

She knew that, too? Well, well, Mrs. Wexler, news does get around. She reminded me of the gossipy old aunt in books who manages to find out everyone's business.

"I'd appreciate it if you would do it on your way home, as I understand she is planning to leave the city for the holidays."

You didn't have to sound like a baroness-in-training to teach at Corinth. That was Mrs. Wexler's area of expertise.

Most of the teachers were younger, among other things. Mr. Taber, who had my science class, wore acid-washed jeans and sat on the edge of his desk. He dangled one leg, swinging it back and forth. The hypnotic leg, we called it. Zapped scientific thought clear out of your mind.

Taber coached the volleyball team, too – we played a couple of other girls' schools. Our favourite cheer was:

Spencer! Marshall! Start your cryin'.
Corinth beats you without tryin'!

This was a colossal lie. We never won. We collected more zeros than the temperature in Antarctica. That's why we had an underground cheer:

The ball's too big! The net's too tall!
Hey, this ain't tennis – it's volleyball!

When Taber got wind of this cheer he'd admonish us. "School spirit, girls! School spirit!" Even that was kind of sexy.

Mrs. Wexler was loaded with the unsexy school spirit of "old guard" Corinth. At the moment she was also thrusting this manila envelope at me. Would I mind? She had to be joking. In certain situations I'm quite

8

cowardly, and being on scholarship in this very ritzy girls' school is definitely one of them.

"Annabelle, don't you have something to carry it in?"

Obviously I didn't. No hat or gloves, either.

"I don't want it getting wet," she said.

Heaven forbid! I shall protect it with my little remaining body heat.

She watched me slip the envelope under my jacket, got a better grip on her briefcase and then smiled a broad thank-you, which showed as much gums as teeth. The minute she turned to go I called after her, "Merry Christmas, Mrs. Wexler."

She stopped dead in her tracks. "Why, thank you, Annabelle. And a Merry Christmas to you, too." She finished with a twittery laugh, adding, "Don't stay out too long in this terrible weather."

"Right," I muttered as I went down the subway steps. Funny she didn't think of that before sending me on this errand.

As I reached in my jeans pocket for a token, the darn envelope slid out and hit every wet, slushy spot to the bottom. I wiped it with the sleeve of my jacket and tucked it under my arm. If I could freeze to death on the subway platform so could the stupid envelope. My nose began to run. As I rummaged for a tissue, the vibrations of an oncoming train rumbled. Music to my frozen ears.

The other girls at Corinth Academy rode home in limousines or taxis, especially in rotten weather. Well, hey, I did, too. Lots of times – whenever Bernice said, "Hop in, Annie." It made me feel like a charity case.

Still, I never refused. We were both going the same way.

Bernice lived in a luxury high-rise on the edge of Metro Park. I would get out with her and walk over to Tenth Street, where my mother and I lived on the third floor of a four-storey walk-up.

The doorman in Bernice's building announced me on the lobby phone, and I took the elevator up to the eighteenth floor. I had planned to leave the envelope with the doorman. I hadn't seen Bernice around school all day so I figured she'd left for Palm Beach.

The Maxsteads own a condo there. The first cold wind this winter Bernice bent my ear about it. How she loved going there. How she couldn't wait to be where it was warm and sunny. Nice to have choices.

I stepped off the elevator and walked the carpeted hallway to the Maxsteads' door. I could hear voices coming from the apartment, which seemed odd for the middle of a workday. Alma, the maid, answered my knock. Bernice was standing behind her. Right off you could tell she'd been crying. Mascara had dribbled down both cheeks.

"Come on in, Annie," she said with a gloomy smile. The living room was crowded with grown-ups looking as miserable as Bernice. Was this some kind of weird pre-Christmas party or what?

I didn't belong there. "Uh, Bernice, I only came to give you this." I handed her the wet envelope. "It's from Mrs. Wexler. She said to get it to you before you left for Florida."

Bernice shook her head. "We're not going." Her eyes – she has these huge dark eyes – filled with tears. "Come on, Annie, stay. Please. Please."

Usually I ignore Bernice's whining, but I found myself peeling off my soaked jacket and giving it to Alma.

"My God, Annie, your hair is dripping wet. Can I get you a towel?"

Bernice is always noticing little things. She'll stare at whatever she decides to pick on and then make some crack. I shook my head, expecting Niagara Falls. But it was only damp.

"It's hot in here, it'll dry in no time." Since she got me to stay, I came right out and asked, "What's wrong with everyone around here?"

Her face puckered up like a squeezed ball. She led me away from the others, into the dining room, and pulled out a couple of chairs.

Alma and a stranger came through the kitchen door carrying steaming pots of coffee and tea. They went to the far end of the table and set the pots next to plates that had these tiny sandwiches and awesome little cakes on them.

Bernice watched the women leave the room.

"Annie." Her voice was very low.

I leaned forward to hear.

"Annie, Candy is dead."

Words and tears came at the same time. The tears rolled down Bernice's cheeks and disappeared.

"Candy? Your cousin?"

Bernice sniffled.

"Candy is dead?"

She was only fourteen. My age. You're not supposed to die when you're fourteen. She went to school in Switzerland. She loved to ski. It flashed in my mind. "A skiing accident?"

Bernice shook her head. "Meningitis."

Goose bumps crawled up my arms. "She was sick? How come you never said anything? She didn't look sick when she was here for Thanksgiving. Remember? We all went to the record store, and ... "

"Annie, no one knew she was sick. She didn't even have a fever or headache or anything. In the morning Brigitte – that's her roommate – kept calling to wake her for class. Candy didn't move – it was, like, a coma. Brigitte ran for help, but –" Bernice heaved a long, gasping kind of sigh and shrugged. "My aunt and uncle went to bring her, uh, the body home. They phoned to say another kid might have meningitis, too. Maybe they'll close the school."

Talking calmed Bernice down, but I really wanted to leave.

"Hey, I'm going to have a sandwich before my relatives devour them all," she said, rolling her eyes. "You have one, too. I'll get us a couple of Cokes."

"Uh-uh, Bernice, I really shouldn't be here."

"Oh, come on, Annie." She was pretty annoyed, so I knew she was getting back to being her usual bossy self.

"Just have a cup of tea, then you can go."

A hot drink did sound good. My socks and sneakers were still damp, and my feet were numb. Besides,

Bernice was already filling the cups. She put a couple of little cakes on plates for us.

"Could I ever pig out on these *petits fours*. If I weren't on a diet."

I sighed wearily. "Bernice, you need to be on a diet about as much as I do. Just stand up straight."

"Ha!" She gazed past me like she was addressing an audience. "Hear that, guys? Words of wisdom from Miss America."

"What's that supposed to mean?" I asked indignantly.

"Well, what can pretty little Annie know?"

"About what?" Her self-satisfied smile really pissed me off.

"Oh, cut the innocent act, Annie."

"Then say what's bugging you."

"This act you put on, pretending you don't know you're pretty."

She'd been saving this bait, and like an idiot, I bit. "I don't think about my looks one way or the other. You're the only one who thinks it's important."

Bernice shrugged. "Just waiting for you to admit it."

"Okay. Some people consider me pretty. Happy? You're the one who's hung up on looks."

"You found me out!" She feigned shock.

"Fine. You admit it." My turn to get on her case.

Except she sounded pretty complaisant for Bernice.

"I can't help it. It's all my mother and her friends talk about," she explained. "Their nose jobs, their face lifts, their capped teeth, their tummy tucks – pick a body part, it's been renovated." She grimaced. "My mother keeps telling me I'm going to be stunning when I get my nose job this summer. Think she'll kick me out if I'm not?"

Her sarcasm was making me uncomfortable. I took a last bite of *petit four* as Mrs. Maxstead came into the room.

She inspected the table and smoothed an invisible wrinkle in the perfectly starched cloth. Then she lined up the silver in exact rows. Finally she turned and smiled at Bernice. The capped teeth were blinding.

"I'm so glad to see you eating something, darling. I haven't been able to put a bite of food in my mouth since we heard the terrible news. I suppose Bernice told you what happened." She didn't look at me.

"Yes, Mrs. Maxstead. I'm so sorry."

Mrs. Maxstead fascinates me. I'd never once seen her without makeup or with one hair out of place. Even when she wasn't going in to work at the Maxsteads' advertising agency she looked like she was about to hold a press conference.

When my mother wears makeup it's an event. And as soon as she gets home from work she's into jeans and lets down her hair. My mother's hair is really curly. It has that look kids at school pay a fortune for.

Mrs. Maxstead breezed by. She has a walk – tall and proud – that makes you notice her. Grown-ups probably think she's attractive, but to me she seems like hard plastic.

Her perfume made me sneeze. She turned very quickly and glared from the other end of the room. "If

14

you have a cold, Annabelle, you shouldn't be out spreading germs."

I was about to apologize when Bernice laughed self-consciously. "Mother, Annie gave one little sneeze."

I wish she'd just kept quiet.

"Nevertheless," Mrs. Maxstead said disapprovingly, "her hair is wet, her sneakers are wet – "

I looked down at my feet to see if I had messed the carpet.

" – and I should think, Bernice, that after the tragedy that has befallen this family you shouldn't have to be reminded how quickly and unsuspectedly illness can strike."

Bernice just sat there looking guilty.

Mrs. Maxstead picked up a batch of letters from the desk and waved them at Bernice. "When did the mail arrive, and why was it brought in here? I've told Alma a dozen times to leave it on the hall table."

"Daddy likes her to leave it on the desk," Bernice mumbled.

"He's quite aware that it doesn't make any sense to carry it back here. I want to see it when I come through the door. And don't talk with your mouth full, Bernice."

The One Who Rules. That described Mrs. Maxstead. She had never asked me a personal question. Not out of politeness, either. But as if she already knew more than she cared to, and none of it pleased her. I always felt awkward when she was around, like she really wished Bernice wouldn't invite me over. As if I weren't good enough.

She was skimming one of the letters. "Tickets for the Corinth Founder's Day Ball are up again this year. Next they'll probably raise the tuition."

"Count on it." Bernice grinned. "Corinth has to hold on to its rep as a school for rich kids."

"If the families happen to be affluent and important, Bernice, that doesn't detract from Corinth's reputation for superior academic standing. You may recall its stiff entrance examination."

Recall it? Just mentioning it was enough to give me a major heart attack. That morning last winter was a clone of this one. The subways got delayed because the tracks were frozen, and when I finally got to the school the furnace had conked out. We were allowed to keep our jackets on, but it was my fingers I could hardly get to move. Corinth is ancient. My mother calls the building shabby-genteel. She says the only thing holding up the plaster is tradition.

When we got the exam results only one other scholarship was awarded. To Carrie Lim.

I gave Bernice a sideways glance. She'd tuned out on Mrs. Maxstead's ad campaign for Corinth. "You should both be extremely proud to be Corinth girls. You especially, Annabelle, as I understand you're there on a full scholarship. You might bear in mind that it's the parents of paying students who provide opportunities for scholarship girls through sizeable tuition."

Why did I have this stupid smile on my face?

"Mother," Bernice began, "Annie got the highest entrance – "

Oh, no. Bernice was coming to my defence again.

Except Mrs. Maxstead wasn't paying the slightest attention. She was inspecting the table as if she were in charge of a state dinner.

"I'm calling everyone in now, Bernice, so will you clear all this ... this litter." She waved her hands over the table. Apparently we'd dropped a few crumbs.

"And please, not on the floor." On her way out she stopped abruptly, turned and eyed me in a more than usually peculiar way. "Annabelle, you and Candy were about the same size, weren't you?"

The question sort of surprised me. "Well, uh, yes, I guess we were."

"Wait here." It was an order.

As soon as her back was to us I signalled to Bernice – what's that all about? But Bernice just shrugged and began sweeping the crumbs from the table into the palm of her hand, then licked them up like a puppy.

"Bernice, that's disgusting."

"I know," she said.

Mrs. Maxstead came back carrying this huge cardboard box. "Annabelle," she said, walking over to me, "I want you to have this. I meant it for Candy's Christmas, but – " She stopped to regain her composure.

I couldn't look at her – I kept my eyes glued to the box, reading the name on it over and over. Mannerheim's. About the most expensive store you could set foot in.

Now she was pushing the box at me. "Please take it!"

She pushed it against me so hard I automatically stepped back. She moved with me. "Just get it out of my sight!"

I took the box and almost dropped it. It was heavier than I expected. "Mrs. Maxstead, in case it doesn't fit shall I – "

She sliced the air with her hands so her bracelets clanked against each other.

"Oh, dear God, I don't care what you do with it. That sweet, precious child. It's too painful." She brushed past me and out of the room. Bernice was crying again.

After a minute I whispered, "Well, I better go now." She nodded. I glanced into the living room as I passed. Joan, Bernice's older sister, threw me a weak smile. I smiled back, got my jacket from Alma and left.

Once outside the door I began wondering what was inside the box. I knew the Maxsteads loved to spend money. Shopping was practically a career with Bernice.

Like one time we were walking by this boutique. Bernice saw these great looking T-shirts with logos on them. Just like that she plopped down a hundred bucks. Well, actually she used a credit card. Her mother's.

I remember it gave me a weird feeling – I don't know, like we were strangers. Now here I was with the box holding – well, who knows.

And all because Candy and I were about the same size.

I'm quite tall for fourteen. Bernice is tall, too, but she's two years older, and bigger. Some kids make fun of her but it's not because of her looks. It's how she acts. I mean like she'll bump into someone and then make out like it's their fault. Once, after she almost knocked the books out of a girl's arms, I heard a group snicker and chant:

The mega-klutz – Bernice the Dip

Her face could *sink* a thousand ships.

Bernice brings it on herself, but some kids can be real mean.

I guess we really became friends because we both live downtown. Most Corinth girls live in the classy apartment buildings near the school.

Anyhow, the first week of school Bernice found out we both went home the same way and latched on to me. I didn't know anyone yet, so it was okay with me. I had worried all summer that no one would even talk to me, but the kids bent over backward to show me how very democratic and fair-minded they were.

I felt great everyone being friendly and including me in their plans. Then I realized that hanging out with them took money. So being invited was kind of meaningless. I never said *why* I couldn't go – just, "Can't make it," nothing specific. I knew they'd soon stop asking. Just get tired or bored. In a way it would be a relief. Still, being left out would hurt.

I wondered how I looked walking away from Bernice's building. I carried the box with the Mannerheim's label facing out. The letters were printed in gold, with a red star for the apostrophe. The box was this elegant grey with thick, twisted-rope handles. Talk about impressive!

I noticed boxes people carried and sort of sized up who they might be, carrying a box or bag from a really fancy store. I liked being seen with the Mannerheim's box.

Okay, Annie Lang, what are you doing? Acting like you actually *bought* something in Mannerheim's. Parading with the gold letters facing out to the world. Hey, look at me, everyone! Then I shook my head. Around here fancy labels were as common as doormen. No one would even notice a Mannerheim's box in *this* neighbourhood. So much for pretending I'm something I'm not. I'd gotten so caught up with the impression I was making, I'd forgotten why I was even carrying whatever was inside the box. I'd forgotten all about Candy.

Going home I pass Sutter's Square, lined with boutiques. It's where the Metro Park people do their local shopping. I bet if I stepped into one of them, my Mannerheim's box would have the sales help fawning all over me. Weird.

Right now, in Spin A Yarn's window, they have a sweater I practically shed tears of joy over every time I stop to gaze at it. When someone buys it, I'll die. Just because I can't afford it, the idea of it on someone else's back destroys me.

It's one of my favourite colors. Pale, pale yellow, like butter. They have it displayed with an enormous brown wool shawl, edged with long black fringe, hanging, just barely, from one shoulder. The whole thing's tremendous.

Why do I torture myself? Why don't I rush by Spin A Yarn's without glancing in the window? And keep from yearning for a buttery yellow sweater I'll never own.

It's hopeless. Even next door at the Parisian Patisserie, the smell comes at you with dollar signs. One of their jam cookies or madeleines eats up a week's allowance. They have the *petits fours* I had at Bernice's in the window. If I had the dough – for their dough, ha! – I'd get one for my mother.

While I stand there drooling, I can hear her saying, "But, Annie, how can they get off charging a small fortune for a loaf of bread? After all, it's only yeast, flour and a little shortening. Even in Metro Park, there's got to be a limit." Then she claims people are capable of promoting the idea of status with anything. If you think about it her way, it is hard to understand, I guess.

By the time I got to Logan Avenue my frozen ears and hands were ready to drop off. I tried holding the box under my arm – at least then I could put both hands in my pockets – only it was too bulky.

Logan is the great divide between the fancy boutiques and the houses – big row houses that run for blocks on both sides of the street.

These old houses are really nice. Used to be when people had lots of kids, a family would have one all to themselves. Now they're broken up into apartments. Carol Breiner, a friend from my public school, lives in one. Of course they're way too expensive for Mom and me, but I'd rather live in one of them than a super-rich high-rise like Bernice's. Which shows how completely practical I can be when weaving my fantasies.

My territory is Twelfth Street. Around here I can go blindfolded. Bargain World, Woolco, Pennysmart. I never look in their windows. Unfortunately, I know every one of their aisles and counters too well. I bet I've walked their floors half the distance to the Equator.

Last Christmas I saw a pair of earrings in Bargain World that I could afford and looked like they might pass for decent. My mother is crazy about earrings, so I got them and felt pretty terrific when she said, "Annie, you have wonderful taste." Seems I had lucked onto a copy of this famous jewellery designer, Katrina Rusearosa. My mother had seen pictures of her stuff in magazines.

Then what happens? The cheap metal gave her a terrible ear infection. Her lobe blew up like a balloon. It just wouldn't clear up when she tried treating it herself. Finally she had to go to the doctor. "Copy," bull. Fake, phoney, cheap is what they should call them. I wish I'd never have to step into a Twelfth Street store again.

By the time I reached my building, I couldn't feel my toes.

Actually, Bernice and I only live around eight blocks from each other. But sometimes when the weather is lousy, like today, it can seem miles. For this freezing trek home, I can thank Mrs. Wexler. If she hadn't seen me, she'd probably have sent the envelope to Bernice in a cab. But then, of course … the box. I wouldn't have the Mannerheim's box, and whatever it held.

My building is in the middle of the block and looks pretty much like all the others: seedy, dilapidated, near collapse. Still, at least I can thaw out inside.

Enter 832 Tenth Street at your own risk. If you don't know your way, you stand a good chance of breaking your neck. The Flickering Flame, our hall light, is programmed to burn out every other day. But my mother, ever the optimist, says groping in the dark is good training for climbing sure-footed through life.

Who needs to be sure-footed, unless you're a mountain goat? Being able to see where you're *headed*, that's good training for life. But I will admit not being able to see the worn-through linoleum and peeling paint is definitely a plus.

My mother also claims that not having an elevator is good for the legs. Call-Me-A-Taxi Bernice has fabulous legs, and she never walks *anywhere*.

No doorman or elevator, no lobby here. Just a narrow staircase and a stale smell that hits you coming and going. Every step creaked. If I ever got a date and tried to sneak in late – forget it.

I'd walked up almost one flight when Mrs. Deksnis who lives on the top floor came from around the landing, Jaimie in one arm and his stroller on the other. If you leave strollers or anything downstairs, they'll be ripped off.

I moved aside to let her pass, but she moved at the same time, so we blocked each other again. I moved back – she did, too – and we did that little dance.

We started to laugh, and I stood still so that she could continue down. It broke the ice. For several weeks now things had been kind of tense when we met in the hallway.

Helen and Nick Deksnis still owed me six bucks from when I last baby-sat for them weeks ago. They're both actors and had auditions for the same afternoon. I don't think I would have minded – well, maybe not quite so much – except that they didn't mention they were short of money until after they came back. Then they asked very sweetly would I mind waiting to be paid.

Of course I minded.

Oh, I'll be paid eventually. Except with Christmas practically here I could really use the money.

As I brought the box into my room, the phone rang.

"Annie?"

For a second I just stood there, stunned. Then I screamed, "Linda?"

She started to giggle.

Linda Wilder was my best friend, until she moved to Bakersville, at the end of last term.

"I'm here, Annie!"

"Where's here? You mean here, right here?"

"Yeah."

"Why didn't you tell me you were coming – you ditz!"

"Hey, we were on our way to my grandmother's. We were supposed to drive straight through. But my dad said he wanted to stop off and visit his sister."

"You're at your aunt's? Terrific! Then you can come right over!"

"Uh-uh, Annie, I can't."

"Why not? Just walk out. "

"Sure, Annie. Look, everyone wants to see us, okay?

My aunt sort of arranged a big family reunion. Tomorrow, okay?"

"Make it real early."

"Yeah, I have loads to tell you."

"Juicy stuff, huh?"

"Tomorrow, Annie," she taunted.

"Give me a hint," I pleaded.

"No way," she laughed.

"Okay, so tomorrow morning."

"I have to go now, Annie."

"Linda – " But she had hung up.

Linda and I are both lousy letter writers, but we used to gab for hours on the phone. But when Linda moved a thousand miles away, our mothers drew the line at non-stop calls long distance. So in a way we fell out of touch, but she's still my best friend.

I went into my room – really, an oversized closet – to see what was inside the box.

There were no scissors handy so I yanked at the cord. Very dumb. The darn thing almost sliced my hand in half before it broke. I opened the box. Boy, Mannerheim's had enough tissue paper across the top to stuff a whale.

Underneath was a jacket. Candy may have been at school in Switzerland, but this wasn't exactly meant for the ski slopes. It made me think of a movie: all these sophisticated characters at some mountain lodge with an enormous fireplace, gabbing and looking like they just walked out of a Paris boutique.

I couldn't wait to try it on. Oh, talk about soft. I stood

in front of the mirror hanging behind the door. Um. Not bad. Maybe I wouldn't actually drool over it if I saw it in a store, but the color was pretty terrific. It was a kind of deep, rich red. And it fit perfectly. On my own jacket the sleeves crawl up inches above my wrists because I've outgrown it. And the collar – snug on my neck, like the fur of a kitten. I was so busy looking at myself and posing that the truth took a while to sink in.

I had to face it, though: the jacket was too pretty. It was the exact opposite of trendy. All the girls at Corinth wore throw-away clothes. I mean clothes that were so casual they had a throw-away look. The only thing was, that look cost serious money. In Mrs. Maxstead's jacket I'd stick out like a neon sign.

I took it off and folded it back in the box. No way would I tell my mother. Not that she would want me to wear anything that made me feel, you know, out of place. But every time she saw my jacket she agonized over its being so threadbare. Better not to gamble with a mother's protective instincts. So when I heard her key in the lock, I kicked the untied box under the bed until I decided what to do.

"I'm home, Annie," she called.

"I'll be right there, Mom." I finally slipped on some dry socks and some old sneakers, on which my toes have pushed clear through the canvas, and went into the other room. "Mom, Linda is here," I told her excitedly.

My mother looked around the room. "No, not here." I laughed. "Here in the city."

"Terrific! Is she going to be here for the holiday week?"

"Uh-uh, only for one day."

"You mean I won't get to see her?"

My mother sounded disappointed – she likes Linda. She flicked the radio on. The dial is always set to the classical music station.

I recognized what was being played. It was Schubert's *Eighth*, the "Unfinished Symphony." Sometimes I call it the ninth by mistake. I mean he wrote nine altogether, so it's logical to think the last one would be the one he never finished, right? Wrong.

Anyway, I know it the minute I hear it because my mother used to sort of sing it to me. When she was in school, she had this teacher, in music appreciation, who would put words to themes so the kids would remember them. It sounds dumb, but it works.

It's something like a school cheer. Once it gets inside your head, it sticks.

My mother thinks it's a terrific way to learn all kinds of stuff. Like when I was having trouble remembering nine times seven in multiplication, she rapped this one on me.

"Listen, Annie, and you'll agree,
That nine times seven is sixty-three."

I'll probably never get it out of my head now, even when I don't give a darn about it anymore.

"I wonder if Linda has changed much," my mother asked.

"How much could she change in six months?"

"Annie, sometimes I'll notice something about you that I'm positive was different the night before."

"Yeah, I wake up with a zit on the tip of my nose."

"That, too." My mother gave me this great smile. That's one of the nicest things about her – I mean her smile. It sort of – well, like her whole face opens up.

"Did you make any special plans?"

"No, not yet."

"Why don't you introduce her to some of your new friends?"

"Uh-uh. I don't think Linda would like meeting Corinth types." My mother gave me a raised eyebrow. "You think she would?"

"Why not?"

"Well, Megan O'Sullivan, maybe. But not Stacey Wasserman. She never shuts up. Or – "

"I thought you liked Stacey."

"I do. Only she's so – so hyper. If you don't practically sit on her, you'd never get a word in. And you know how Linda is. She's shy."

"I don't think so."

"No kidding?"

"Really. In fact, when you were in second grade, Mrs. Eberweiss – "

"Eberweiss was third grade, definitely."

"Okay. The important thing is, we happened to meet Linda and Jane in the supermarket, just after Jane's parent interview with Mrs. Eberweiss. She was quite upset with Mrs. E.'s evaluation of Linda."

"Why? Linda's smart. Besides, she was a perfect little angel in class."

"That was the trouble. According to Mrs. Eberweiss she needed to become less reticent and more outgoing."

I shook my head. "Well, she never did. She's still quiet."

"But not shy."

"Well, yeah, she was never weird or anything."

"Exactly. You'd think any teacher would wish for a few quiet children."

"Yeah, especially Eberweiss. Most of us were non-stop motor mouths."

My mother suddenly had this big grin on her face.

"What's so funny?"

"Oh, the way Linda proved my point. Jane and I knew each other from the playground and PTA meetings, and you and Linda were in the same class, but you weren't particular friends.

"So all of a sudden here was Linda begging Jane to let you go over to their house to play. Linda had never asked anyone over before. Jane was so relieved, we laughed over it for years. Whenever Linda did anything the least bit daring – "

"Like the time she cut her hair with a pinking shears?"

My mother gasped. "Punk, before it had been invented."

I nodded.

"Jane would be on the phone with, 'Guess what the reticent one has done now.' "

"Yeah, we got to be best friends pretty quick. And, Mom, I'm not saying it wouldn't be fun if some of the kids from Corinth joined us tomorrow. But the thing is, Linda isn't going to be here very long. And I want to spend the time with her alone. I mean, we're only going to have a few hours."

"That's fine, Annie. I'm delighted you're going to see her, and disappointed I'm not. But right now I think we better get these groceries put away."

"What did you buy?" I asked, snooping into the bag she had brought.

"Oh, Joe called me at work," she said, carrying her coat and heading into her room – a slightly larger closet. "He's coming, and he's bringing Mathew."

Joe Zucca is my mother's boyfriend, they met at night school. Joe drives a cab during the day, but wants to be an accountant. Mathew, his little boy, has lived with his mother since Joe's divorce a couple of years ago.

"How about this weather turning so nasty," my mother said, coming back. "When I left for work this morning the sun was actually shining."

"Yeah, tell me about it."

"I bet you were freezing, Annie." She had her worried look on.

"Nah, I was fine," I lied. I felt guilty, but there was no way I was going to mention Mrs. Maxstead's jacket. "What smells?"

"Gorgonzola cheese – Mathew's favourite. Yesterday was his birthday. Since Joe has him today I thought we might have a little celebration."

"Boy, if this kid likes Gorgonzola cheese he must really be weird."

"Turnips." My mother gave me a mischievous smile.

"Okay, I apologize," I said, stifling a laugh. When I was around four or five I wouldn't eat vegetables. So my mother went on a crusade. She tried every vegetable going, starting with asparagus and working toward zucchini. I spit them all out. She was running out of alphabet when she came to T – turnips. I loved turnips. What can I say. My mother said she thought turnips would come out our ears.

I took the cheese out of the bag. "If I'd known it was his birthday I might have bought him something."

But the truth is I hadn't let myself get attached to this kid, although he did seem to be a pretty decent little boy. It was better that way – till I was sure about what was going to happen. I mean between my mother and Joe. Besides, the idea of having a little brother and a father sometimes knocked the breath clear out of me.

Of course, I had a father. Everyone has a father. Just because I'd never even seen him didn't change the fact that we were father and daughter. But for now he's my special secret. Except lots of times I'll think so hard about him, it's like I could almost make him appear.

"It's me, Annabelle," he'd say. Looking long and lean, the way he does in that picture my mother has – they're standing with their arms around each other's waists and looking into each other's smiling eyes. "It's me, Bennett Styles Whittledge, your father."

"Annabelle? What? What's going on?"

"Oh." I grinned, flustered. "Nothing." It's funny. When you feel guilty about your thoughts, you think everyone can read them.

"Wool-gathering?" my mother teased.

"Guess so," I answered, pulling a bottle of wine from the bag of groceries.

"Sweetie, would you mind putting the wine in the fridge to chill, please. And put the rest of the things away. I'd like to take a quick shower before I start dinner. Okay?"

"Sure," I said, realizing how I seemed to be developing the same walk she has. We both took sort of loping steps.

Otherwise I didn't think we looked anything alike. Her hair, she told me, used to be dark blonde like mine when she was younger. But ever since I can remember it's been brown. The shape of her face is longer than mine and her features more pronounced. Still, when we're in a store together someone is bound to say, "Oh, Mrs. Lang, I'd know this was your daughter anywhere. You look exactly alike. They all say *Mrs.* Lang, but Bettina, my mother, isn't a Mrs. Never was.

I carried the rest of the groceries through the archway into the kitchen. We could hang up a curtain to separate the kitchen and living room, but we never got around to it.

I fluffed the pillows on the sofa and ran the sweeper. As I was putting it away the bell rang. It was too early for Joe and Mathew. Maybe Linda got away after all. I rushed over and shouted into the intercom, "Linda?" But it wasn't her.

It took a minute for my disappointment to pass before I was conscious of the impatient voice at the other end.

"Annie, buzz me in!"

"Bernice?"

"Yeah!"

Well, it wasn't what I'd hoped for, but I was still surprised. I kind of just stood at the intercom until Bernice screamed in my ear.

"Come on, Annie, buzz me in!"

Bernice doesn't come over often and never without calling first. I'd just left her a little while ago. Besides, I didn't want her here when Joe and Mathew arrived. I didn't want anyone from school to know too much about my life.

There's a side of Corinth the One Who Rules doesn't have a clue about. The place is a gossip mill.

Kids just seemed to be able to smell out the dirt. Once they got a peek at a part of your private life – forget it. I mean, they not only gossip about other kids' parents fighting or divorcing, but their own. If dear Mom or Dad were alcoholic or running around, they'd pass the information around like a joint in the john.

When I get asked about my parents I don't actually lie. I duck it – get vague – giving the impression they've been divorced practically since the day I was born and that I rarely see my father. A single-parent home is hardly a novelty, but I'm not sure everyone buys my story, especially Bernice.

Bernice. The jacket. She's coming up to see the jacket. Or to snoop out what was in the box. She'll expect me to try it on and get carried away. I can't deal with this. My mother will – oh, hell.

Only nothing of the kind was on Bernice's mind. She

charged into the apartment and breezed by me like I was the doorman in her building. Her expression was foul.

"God, my mother pisses me off. I had to get out of there. I didn't tell her where I was going. Not that she gives a damn."

Hardly the heart-broken Bernice I'd left earlier. She took off her things without even asking if it was okay to stay, then threw her stuff all over the sofa I had just tidied.

Plopping down on top of her jacket, she stretched her legs out in front of her, hitting against the coffee table and blocking a pathway.

"Oh, hello, Mrs. Lang."

My mother came into the room. Her hair was down, her cheeks pink from the bathroom steam. In her shirt and jeans she didn't look much older than us.

"Bernice, hello," she said. "We haven't seen you around here in quite a while." Then she turned to face me. "Annie, I have to run down to the store for a few more things." She spoke slowly with the faintest of smiles. I got the message: don't let Bernice stay too long.

The second my mother closed the door behind her Bernice went into her usual tirade. Her mother favoured her sister, Joan, made excuses for Joan's behaviour, on and on.

I had heard all this a million times before. Why was it so urgent? Then she blurted out what really brought her here.

"Annie, I have a date! It's with Jimmy Lassiter. You

know, the boy I told you about from camp last summer. He called me right after you left."

"No kidding." There was practically no part of her life that Bernice hadn't given me every detail of. And I knew she'd never been asked out on a date. "Hey, that's great." I was really happy for her.

"Not so great." She was pouting again. "My mother won't let me go."

Bernice was constantly complaining, which could be a colossal pain. Still, she had such a lousy opinion of herself I couldn't understand Mrs. Maxstead not letting her go.

"Why?" I went into the kitchen for the place-mats.

"Because," Bernice said, still surly. "Because of Candy."

I was shocked. "You want a date on the day of the funeral?"

"Of course not," Bernice snarled. "He asked me for the day after Christmas." Her face broke into an enormous grin. "Annie, he hinted about New Year's Eve, too. I can't believe it. An honest-to-goodness date for New Year's." She pounded her heels against the floor like a two-year-old. The people downstairs must have loved it.

"So why won't your mother let you go?" I had started to set the table and was moving around.

"You know," she said, screwing up her nose and imitating her mother's way of talking, " 'It's not respectful to Auntie Kate and Uncle Jack.' Bull! What damn difference does it make to them? Is turning down a date going to make them feel better? Besides, Candy would

35

want me to go. I told my mother, too."

I was making a big show of arranging everything on the table very carefully, almost worthy of Mrs. Maxstead. I was hoping Bernice would take the hint something was going on.

But Bernice just kept going. "My mother's the one who's always bitching that I'm never asked out." She shifted her weight and pulled her jacket out from under her. All right, a move to get up. But, no, she just dumped the jacket on her lap. "She keeps on at me about how popular Joan was at my age. Ha! If she only knew."

Bernice claimed her sister had slept with half the boys in her high-school class, but I didn't believe it. After all, Bernice had also told me that last summer she "did it" with some boy. Later she changed her story – they almost did, but not quite.

Now she was getting really comfortable, sprawling all over the sofa.

"First she tells me I should be going out. Then she tells me how gorgeous I'll be after I get my nose job. So what's the message? Huh, Annie? I'm ugly, right?"

She stretched her neck forward like a chicken. "Maybe I won't get a nose job. Serve her right if she has to look at my ugly face for the rest of her life."

"Oh, Bernice, for heaven's sake." I was getting really tired of all this. "You're not ugly. It's dumb to be so hung up on looks."

"Right. You can talk."

"Come on, Bernice. It's just as stupid for someone who's, uh, pretty."

"Well, excuse my ass. A fourteen-year-old philosopher."

I took a deep breath. "Look, Bernice, we're expecting company. You'll have to excuse me, but I have things to do for my mother now."

For the first time Bernice seemed to notice what was going on around her. She gathered up her things, then put them on.

"Funeral's tomorrow."

"Maybe it won't be too awful." Who was I kidding?

"Annie, it's hard to believe I won't ever see her again."

I didn't know what to say. I walked with her to the door and wondered if she would ask about the box. All she said was, "Look, I'll call you, okay? We'll get together."

A few minutes later my mother came back.

"What did Bernice want? Anything special?"

"She's having a rough time. Her cousin died."

My mother had a confused look. "Who?"

"Her cousin. You never met her." I didn't see any point in it. If I told her what happened, I could trap myself, and I had already decided to give the jacket back to the One Who Rules.

CHAPTER TWO

I WAS CURLED UP ON THE SOFA sort of reading a book, but not really into it.

My mother was bending over the stove. Once I made her laugh when I called her the Whirling Dervish, the way she'd whirl around from one thing to the next.

Oh, sure, I helped – and had regular chores – but she was the one who kept us on track.

"Mom?"

"Yes, Annie?" She turned and gave me a happy smile. Joe was coming.

"What's that super smell?"

"Oh," she said, "it must be the curry."

That meant we were having a chicken casserole. Joe always got star treatment.

"We got anything for a snack?" Ordinarily I would have grabbed something the minute I set foot in the house. But I got snagged by Bernice's visit.

"Can you hold off, Annie? It shouldn't be too long before they get here. And we have a big dinner."

"Need any help?"

"Nope, all set."

She came in and sat down next to me, leaning her head against the headrest. "When is Bernice leaving for Florida?"

"They're not going. You know – because of the funeral."

My mother nodded. She looked at me and smiled. "Bernice reminds me so much of a girl in my high-school class."

"She does?" Could there be another one?

"She was the same age as most of us, but bigger." My mother made a wide circling motion out from her bosom.

"Bernice doesn't have a big bust," I protested.

"That's not what I meant, exactly. The thing about this girl – her name was Vera – was that she seemed uncomfortable in her own skin."

"Yeah, you're right about that. Bernice is so self-conscious. The worst. She acts like she's the ugliest thing on earth."

"Sometimes a girl like Bernice with very strong features grows into a very interesting-looking woman."

"Mother, please. No girl wants to hang in until she's middle-aged to work up to 'interesting.' "

"Yes, I know, but – "

"Besides, she's getting her nose fixed."

"Is that what she wants?"

"It's what her mother wants."

"You know the magazine that comes from the supermarket? I think I left it on one of the kitchen chairs. Would you mind, Annie?"

She leafed through till she found a page showing some tall, big-boned lady, dressed in black from head to toe and wearing this enormous black picture hat. There was a profile shot of her, too, with the hat off. She had her dark hair pulled back tight from her face in some sort of a knot at her neck. These silver earrings she had on were awesome. Now there's a Christmas present for my mother! Ha!

"Look at this, Annie."

I did. "What?"

"Can't you see?"

I squinted at the picture.

"It's the way she's deliberately playing up her large features. Well, maybe not playing them up, but she's not downplaying them either."

"That's for sure." Her lipstick was so bright it could stop traffic.

My mother was smiling, eyes glued to the picture. "Well, it's obvious she hasn't tried to make herself into some physical type she can never be. That's probably what makes her so ... so arresting."

It was weird. This lady was no beauty, yet she was – uh – great looking. I could see why she made my mother think of Bernice.

"Yeah, but, Mom, look at the way she's standing. Bernice slumps like she's trying to disappear into the ground. Hey, I could show this to Bernice. It'll change her life." My mother missed the sarcasm.

"Sure. I'm through with it." Suddenly she jumped up from the sofa. "Oh, Annie, the cheese. I meant to leave it out at room temperature."

I closed the magazine. "You know, Mom, some kids at school are real snotty to her."

"And ... to you, Annie?"

"Me? Oh, no! Except for a few first-class snobs who are that way to everybody. There is one thing, though." I decided to go for it. "Who your family is and what your parents do matters a lot. The first day, Letitia Taylor asked me if my father was Dr. Lang."

"Who?" My mother had her worried look on her face.

I tried to make it sound unimportant. "There's this very tony dermatologist named Lang. He gets all the rich kids' pimples. I told her no. But hey, what if I had told her my father was Bennett Styles Whittledge. That would have been something else, huh?"

My mother had turned into the kitchen and was ignoring me – like she usually did when I got on the topic. It was as if it were a part of her life that didn't matter. Well, it did to me. "Well, Mom? Tongues would wag, wouldn't they?"

She didn't answer me.

"Mother?"

Slowly she turned away from the sink and stood in the archway. Her voice was very subdued. "Must you bring this up now, Annie?"

"What's wrong with now?"

41

"Don't play games with me, Annabelle. Whenever Joe is coming over or he and I are going out you bring up the subject of your father."

"This has nothing to do with Joe. I have the right to ask about my father if I want to. Maybe, one of these days, I'll even get an answer."

Not this time. First I heard a clash of pans. The refrigerator door opened, then shut with a bang. Then there was the sizzle of fat in a pan.

I must have gotten her pretty upset to be hiding it in all that activity. Well, I was pretty upset myself.

"What are you doing?" I asked, trying to sound natural.

"Making palatschinken," she answered in a like tone.

"Why do you always call them palatschinken? Why don't you say crêpes or pancakes?"

She passed me a gracious smile. "I didn't realize it bothered you, Annie."

"It's not that. Anyway, why are you making them now? Joe always brings dessert. Won't they be here soon?"

"Yes, so why don't you help me? You can peel the apples and – "

"I know what to do," I said, a little short. I was having a hard time pretending everything was fine between us.

My mother ignored my edgy tone. "Well, I guess I call them palatschinken because my mother did – and my grandmother. Grandma Lang was half German and half French."

"So she could have called them crêpes just as easily, couldn't she?"

My mother continued to disregard my contrariness. I handed her the peeled apples. "You got these slices perfect, Annie, nice and thin."

I watched her put them in the sugared water to simmer for a few minutes, until they were just transparent. Talk about transparent, I could see right through her act, pretending as if her dropping our discussion didn't bother me.

"So why call them palatschinken? I like French better. French is a romantic language. The French make the best lovers – I've always heard."

"I've always heard it's the Italians," she said, smiling.

But I wasn't ready to make peace. "Well, you should certainly know about that." I could hear how nasty I sounded.

"All right, Annie, why don't you go back to reading or find something else to do."

I wouldn't back down. "How come you had all that time to talk about how Bernice could look but you can't take five minutes to talk about me."

"Because it's not a discussion for five minutes, and now isn't the time."

"It never is," I sulked.

"That's because you keep searching for mystery or intrigue when there's none there."

It wasn't that my mother didn't tell me anything. It was – I don't know – like there had to be more to it all. Maybe in a way she was right. And I did seem to bring him up when Joe was coming. Lately, though, we don't seem to have much time to talk. Three times a week my mother goes to night school to get the rest of the credits she needs for her degree. She works in the Department of Social Services and needs the credits to keep getting promotions.

Sometimes we do homework together and kid each other about who got more. I had English, math, science, the usual required stuff. Then there's my elective major, Latin. Can you believe it? This school still taught Latin. But that's Corinth. And on scholarship you're supposed to be very bright, so it's expected you'll take the tough subjects. In a co-ed school kids probably pick the class with the best guys in it.

Some of the teachers at Corinth boast about graduates who've managed to grab the brass ring out in the world. I think it's totally gross, but I can't deny it's what my mother wants for me. Every so often she'll remind me what a terrific opportunity I have. And to make the most of it. And even if it sounds tacky it's what I want for myself. A scholarship to a top university after Corinth. We talk a lot about it. So I wonder what's the problem. She's totally up front about my future, so why is it so hard for her to find time to talk about my past — our past? My father.

After a while she came over to the window and put her arm around me. She held me for a while, then spoke so softly I had to strain to hear her.

"Annie, I've tried through the years to stick to the things that have meaning for us right now. Does it help anything to go over the what-might-have-beens? Because the fact is, sweetie, the might-have-beens wouldn't have brought us happiness."

"Mom, you can't know that," I protested. "At least I

44

would have had a father."

"A father who gave no indication of wanting us. That's hardly a guarantee of happiness, Annie."

"Well, maybe he was scared. You always say how young he was."

"He didn't stay young forever. Has he ever tried to find us? To know you? Annie, we're not in hiding."

My heart started pounding, racing away from what it didn't need to hear.

"I was young, too," my mother said. "Barely twenty when you were born. Yet even then I knew who I was. What I had to do to look after myself." She shrugged. "Maybe if one of my parents had still been alive, maybe if I had a sister or brother, things might have turned out differently. Only I couldn't dwell on that. Besides, I had done pretty well for myself. I was attending a fine New England college on scholarship."

She smiled. As if to say, " 'See, I'm the one you take after. You don't have to look farther to know who you are.' "

"Annie, I wasn't going to let pity or being ill-used bog me down for the rest of my life. I see plenty of that at work. Women coming in obsessed with finding husbands and fathers. Bitter, paralysed women, neglecting themselves to find someone who doesn't want to be found."

"Did – he – not want to be found?" I couldn't say "Dad" out loud, although I said it lots of times to myself. "I thought his parents didn't want you to get married?"

"At first I was sure it was Mr. and Mrs. Whittledge.

Closer to the time you were due I wasn't so sure."

"But he did love you!" I said fiercely.

"Ah, yes. Love at first sight." Her smile went a little crooked. "I went to a party a friend of mine gave. A boy she knew from Yale brought Ben along. First sight – zap! Dead aim from Cupid's arrow." A light laugh carried her words. "I was wearing this white linen suit – stupidest thing I ever bought. I'd wash and iron the skirt to save money and send just the jacket to the cleaners.

"Anyway, Ben spilled a little wine on the sleeve. He was devastated. The next day he sent me a bouquet of flowers. You wouldn't believe the commotion it caused. No one in the dorm ever got flowers delivered to them. Made quite an impression on a smitten eighteen-year-old."

I loved hearing this. Sure, I needed to know the hard facts, but how they met and all just knocked me out. Real romance. Boy meets girl. "He was really handsome, too, wasn't he?"

"Umn, gorgeous. Fabulous."

"Like in that snapshot we have? He looks awfully young."

She nodded. "Yes, he did. I imagine Ben would always be boyish looking."

We were on a roll. "You said he wasn't going to your college."

"No. Not then. That was the first thing the Whittledges held against me. It was my fault he left Yale."

"Was it?"

"Well, I certainly didn't discourage him when he

decided to transfer to my college. Annie, I was in love."

"And then you started to live together."

"Yes."

My mother claimed it was the same story over and over, but each time some new bit came out.

"You're always talking to me about birth control and learning everything about sex and protecting yourself. You were smart. How come you didn't know?"

"It wasn't that I didn't know, Annie. Nature just has a way of outsmarting us."

I was real careful how I asked her this. "Mom, did you want to – I mean did you do it on purpose because he was super rich?"

"Never. I swear to you, Annie. The money was part of what came between Ben and me. His wealth. Position. Family snobbishness. He was tied to it more deeply than I understood. I thought love conquered all. What did I know about the power of old money?"

I thought it was dumb for her to quit when she only had a little more than a year of college left. And I could have been born there. Maybe she could have forced the Whittledges to accept me – or at least help with some of their spare change. Maybe even force my father to marry her. "You got shafted."

"So you've said."

Well, it was a change from her usual lecture about someday I'd understand that an independent spirit was a force of its own. But all that really happened was she ended up back here, where she claimed she had friends and knew the system better.

The system – ha! Welfare. There's lots we don't see

eye to eye on when it comes to the Whittledges and might-have-beens.

The refrigerator clicked on. The kitchen was warm and smelled sweet from the palatschinken – I guess I'll call them that, too.

I glanced out at the crumbling buildings on Tenth Street. My mother's ambitious, independent spirit had brought us only so far. She liked to say it was good to spend a bit on enjoyment and fun. And bad to dwell on your low economic state. It was a big joke because we seldom had any extra to spend. Oh, sure, once in a blue moon we'd go out to a restaurant. Or to the theatre for a special occasion. And all the free concerts and plays in town.

But Bernice went to camp practically every summer and had been to Europe twice. Everyone at school had been to Europe at least once. And one girl in my class had a family villa in the south of France.

Is that what being at snooty Corinth Academy was doing to me? Did I want to belong there not just because of my scholarship, but because I was Annabelle Imogene Whittledge as much as I was Annie Lang, the daughter of an underpaid civil servant? The possibility made me feel sick.

The doorbell rang, and my mother went to buzz them in. I didn't feel much like company. Not that Joe was company, but I guess I'd have to entertain Mathew.

The only other little kids I knew were Linda's brothers, who were always barging into her room when we wanted to be alone. They were a royal pain. Now, if you couldn't get along with your own family, how could you cope when you got connected through marriage?

Marriage was on my mind a lot lately. My mother could end up marrying Joe Zucca. It was fine for her to love him and, okay, I did like him right off. But the idea of his moving in on us or becoming important in my life gave me a queasy feeling in the pit of my stomach.

The only other guy my mother ever dated steadily was Charles Hermann. He was a cousin of my mother's closest friend, Lisa Hermann, from work. I was eleven then and thought Charles Hermann was gorgeous. He was tall and built like an athlete and had lots of white teeth. Now that I think of it, they were a lot like Mrs. Maxstead's porcelain dazzlers.

After a few months of Charles Hermann my mother decided that the chances of falling in love with him were zilch, and he was gone. I was ecstatic. Joe Zucca is only medium tall and wiry. He has an okay face. Nice.

I stepped out of the kitchen when Joe and Mathew came into the apartment. We were a chorus of hi's back and forth. Then I whizzed Mathew into my room. I figured my mother would appreciate that.

"Can I help you off with your things, Mathew?"

"Hey, do I look like a baby?"

"Yep."

"Well, I'm not!" He yanked his stuff off and threw it on the bed.

I took a book from the stack on the table where I do my homework. He plopped down on the floor.

"You had a birthday, didn't you?"

"Yesterday. I was six years old. Told you I wasn't a baby."

"Okay. See this book?"

"Yeah?"

"Well, it's for you." He looked up at me with his china-blue eyes, crinkled his nose and smiled. Definitely a cute-looking kid.

"It is?"

"Uh-huh. A birthday present."

"Thank you." He glanced at the cover. "Will I like it?"

"Oh, sure. It's a terrific story. This selfish giant gets changed into a little child because he does a kind thing. Open it. It has lots of pictures." When I said pictures he looked around the room.

"Hey, where's the TV?"

"Remember when you were here the last time, I told you it was broken."

"You didn't get it fixed yet?"

"Nope."

"How come?"

I shrugged. "Too expensive, I guess."

"Ours broke and my mother got it fixed right away. Wanna come over and watch?"

Terrific. "Well, thank you, Mathew, but I think we'll get ours fixed soon."

"There's no window in here. How can you see out?"

"I have a window in my head," I said.

He broke into a full laugh. "No, you don't!"

He looked a lot like Joe when he did that. I couldn't help grinning.

My mother called us in to dinner.

Joe had the radio playing softly in the background. Opera. Once I told my mother that of all the times I'd been in taxis with Bernice, no driver was ever listening to opera. She said I shouldn't stereotype people.

When we were all seated around the table, Mathew said, "Dad, aren't you going to tell me what happened today, like you promised?"

"Uh-huh. I didn't forget."

"Was it something real weird, Dad?"

"Is this going to be one of your off-the-wall stories?" my mother asked with a suspicious grin.

Joe raised his arms in protest, his face bathed in mock innocence. "How could you think that? No, this is an award winner. An Oscar among taxi tales. Scratch that. We're talking hard facts here. Reality. Substance."

"Don't forget 'insight,' " my mother teased.

"I like the one you told last time we were here."

"Which one was that, Matty?"

"You know, about the dead body."

"Oh," I groaned, "the travelling cadaver story."

"Well, Mathew, that wasn't exactly a true story."

"It wasn't?"

"Not completely."

"About ninety-nine per cent made up, Mathew." I grinned.

Joe passed me a mock hurt expression. "Come on, Annie, as I recall you got a big kick out of it."

"It wasn't the story – it was your winning performance."

"Dad, you know what part I liked best? Where the

man jumps into the cab and shouts, 'Follow that car!' Did you, Annie?"

"Uh-uh, I liked the part where Joe tells the guy he's on delivery. How he has a corpse in the trunk that he has to rush to the city morgue."

"Hey, you guys. It was past two o'clock. I hadn't eaten since six that morning except for one quick cup of disgusting coffee from a cart. I had to get rid of this passenger before I died of starvation."

"So why didn't you put up your off-duty sign?" I asked.

My mother was laughing. "You're all acting as if any of this actually happened."

"It did," Mathew said, cracking Joe and me up, too.

The chicken casserole was dished out and passed around the table.

"Betts, this is — " Joe gave her a thumbs up.

My mother beamed. Joe beamed back.

"I like it, too, Betts. It's good."

"Why, thank you, Matt."

"It tastes almost the same as the kind my mommy makes."

Goodbye, magic moment. There was this real awkward silence all of a sudden. But I guess little kids don't notice, because Mathew was yanking on Joe's sleeve, a big grin on his face.

"Hey, Dad, guess what? Annie gave me a book for my birthday. It's about a giant who gets turned into a little child because he does a kind thing. Right, Annie?"

"Uh-huh."

"Oh, Annie!" My mother was really pleased. Mathew had obviously cleared the air. "You gave him your Oscar Wilde."

"Well, someone's got to give the kid a bit of culture," I joked.

Joe put on this real corny accent like an old cowboy movie star. He cleared his throat. "Well, now there, missy. I'm acquainted with the infamous Mr. Wilde. You smart young 'uns are all alike. Get to thinkin' we older folk reside on some remote planet."

"I'm a smart young 'un, too, Dad," Mathew said.

"You bet!" He reached over and gave him a big hug. Then looked at me. "You, too, Annie."

I smiled. But it kind of made me uncomfortable. Joe's always friendly to me. Well, hey, I'm friendly, too. Only this was different – affectionate. When I saw my mother's face light up, I was sure. As if when Joe said it to me, he had handed her the world. Boy, was it getting cosy around here.

"Dad, you're not telling us what happened today, like you promised."

"I will. But don't you think we should give undivided attention to this wonderful dinner Betts made?"

Careful, Joe, I mumbled to myself. Stay off the eats. Or Mathew may do another comparative test taste.

"The salad's delicious, Mom." I could hardly believe how the words slipped out – almost at the same time as my silent warning to Joe. Did I do it on purpose? Hoping Mathew would put his foot in it again. Tell us his mother's salads were good, too. I didn't know. It was the way they kept looking at each other. I wanted to think, how totally disgusting – but somehow, I couldn't.

"Don't keep him waiting, Joe. If you promised, tell him what happened," my mother said.

"Okay, you have to trust me," Joe's left hand went over his heart, while he raised his right. "True. Every last word."

"Does this one have a dead body in it, Dad?"

"No, Matty, just dead weight."

There was no escape.

"Well, the morning wasn't great. The minute I hit the street, I knew the Board of Taxi Officialdom was on the prowl."

"Were the taxi cops after you, Dad?"

"Who knows what they were after? Overdue license registration? Illegal aliens driving?" Joe shrugged. "Anyway, about four o'clock, I headed down to the stock exchange as the floor traders were leaving. Sure enough, a cop flagged me down."

"Oh, Dad, you got a ticket."

"No, I thought I was going to, except I couldn't imagine for what."

"For the cadaver in the trunk," I suggested. Joe laughed.

"Annie, don't interrupt," my mother protested. "I have to keep alert against digressions from the truth."

Joe winked at her. I couldn't figure out why, but it meant something. People just don't wink for no reason.

"Well, the cop came up to me and says, 'I have a passenger for you.' I look over his shoulder, and sure enough, getting out of a limo parked at the corner, is Walter Branton."

"The politician?"

Boy, was my mother impressed.

"Yep, in the flesh. Seems his limo conked out. He was due at a press conference and he was late. So he parks himself in the back seat of my cab. Turned on the charm and got very friendly, he thought. He'd ask my opinion on something, and when I'd start giving it to him, he'd talk right over me."

"Joe, what did he want your opinion on?"

My mother was acting like a wide-eyed teenager. It was embarrassing.

"They've got this bill pending on shelters for boys getting out of detention. They're setting up a halfway house so the kids can readjust for a while, instead of turning them back out on the street. As usual everyone's crying, 'Not in my backyard.' You know, property values going down and all that."

"How about Walter Branton's backyard?"

"Exactly, Annie, how about it? Most people are pretty fair-minded. There'd be less belly-aching if every district took its share. I'd have told that to Branton, too, if he'd given me the chance."

Mathew was pouting. "Aw, Dad, this isn't a funny taxi story."

"The funny part's coming now, Matt."

Joe turned to my mother. "When we stopped, he studied the meter real hard and asked me if it read five fifty. Even after I told him, he leaned forward like he was trying to see and asked me again. This time I kind of shouted it, thinking maybe he was hard of hearing. Still he didn't budge. All I was getting was a big grin. I was also beginning to get the idea.

"He could tell I owned the cab, and he wanted a free ride. Because he wanted it so bad, I decided not to give it to him. If he had offered to pay, I might have said, 'Privilege to serve you, sir, the ride's on me.' But now, no way. So he counts out five singles and five dimes and walks away."

"He fleeced you out of a tip!"

"Lucky I didn't get the whole tab in pennies. What you learn about human nature driving a cab, you can't learn anywhere else."

"Then maybe that's what I'll do after I graduate from college," I said, getting a laugh.

"Aw, gee, Dad, I didn't like that story. I like the kind with car crashes, and sirens, and dead bodies."

"I know, Matty. But we've got to try other things once in a while."

"You'd think," my mother said, "he'd take better care of his image. He just doesn't give a damn. Arrogant pig. Who does he think put him in office? Well – " She got up to clear the dishes. Joe jumped up to help her before I could. He always did that. It scored points with my mother, but it made me uncomfortable. Like maybe he was a bit too much at home. Instead of behaving like a guest. And tonight he seemed more at home than ever.

When the table was cleared they brought in the palatschinken and the kirschwasser that you pour over them to get them to ignite.

"What's that?" Mathew asked as my mother started to pour the kirschwasser.

"It's stuff made from black cherries," I told him.

"Then how come it's white?" he asked suspiciously. "Doesn't look white to me."

My mother smiled but shook her head. She didn't approve of my teasing him. Then she doused the lights and handed me the matches.

We all watched the blue flame burst bright into the room.

"Oooh," Mathew squealed. "Oooh, look!"

Everyone applauded. Then with the coffee my mother served the Gorgonzola cheese and crackers, which she set down in front of Mathew. It turned out to be a pretty nice birthday. If my mother hadn't gotten mad enough to start banging around the pots and pans, dessert would probably have ended up being ice cream and cookies.

Joe moved back from the table and sighed. "Great dinner, Betts."

I wondered if anyone would ever smile at me that way. Or if my face would light up at the sight of someone, the way their faces did.

Actually I did meet someone I like. At a party. Hey, where else do you meet boys when you go to an all-girls school.

Anyway, Megan O'Sullivan's brother Sean had a party for his sixteenth birthday last month. He goes to an all-boys school, so he invited three of us from Corinth. Stacey Wasserman, Rosemary Heffington and me.

I'd only met him once before, when he stopped by

after school one day to meet Megan. She and I were talking on the school steps.

This was no ordinary run-of-the-mill birthday party. Brunch at his place on a Saturday morning. Eggs Benedict. Caviar, which of course I'd never tasted but didn't admit it. All kinds of croissants and sweet buns, jams and cheeses. What a pig out. You'd think we were starving to death.

We all got along pretty well, and the talk was easy and friendly. Some of it had to do with parents, like when Sean said to Stacey Wasserman, "Who screwed up on your father's broadcast last night? How could he get it wrong?"

Syd Darby chimed in, "Yeah, what a glitch."

Stacey's father is a sports broadcaster on TV, and something about a basketball score was open to question.

Then Josh Morgenstern asked Rosemary Heffington if she could get some information for him. Rosemary's mother is a senator, and Josh needed it for a politics report.

I could have told them a dozen stories from the department where my mother is a social worker, only I didn't want to bring up what my mother did. Not because I thought they'd look down on me. Just the opposite. I'd probably get more of that eager showing of acceptance. As if they really knew anything about it.

That's one thing I'll say for Bernice. She never acts solicitous toward me. Maybe that's why she's the one person from Corinth who's been to our apartment. I bet she goes home and says, "Boy, do they live in a dump." Which of course is the truth. Someone like Megan and the others would say, "Oh, it's so sad." To show how their kind hearts are hurting.

After brunch, we were taken by limo to a matinée of a musical. At some point during the show Sean took my hand. Megan had told me Sean kept asking her about me after we had met on the school steps.

What could she have told him? Except that I was on a full scholarship. Full scholarships are given only to qualified students who can prove economic hardship. I wonder if she even understands what the words mean.

Bernice Maxstead's apartment used to be the most luxurious I'd ever seen outside of the movies. Until the day of Sean's party. Once, since then, Sean called me. I got the feeling that the next time he does, he's going to ask me to go someplace with him.

What would he think of our apartment? My mother would say if he really likes you it won't matter. My mother, of all people! More than likely she only says that so I won't feel ashamed of the fact that our building is one step up from a tenement.

Well, stick with your own kind doesn't just mean ethnic.

Joe and my mother were kissing. They didn't mind if anyone saw them. Mathew kicked his feet against the chair. "Mushy stuff," he said, like something tasted awful.

"Okay, champ," Joe said, "I better get you back home or your mother will feed me to the lions."

"I'll get his things," I said, and went into my room.

59

Joe manages to see his kid. Half the kids in my class have divorced parents, and they see their fathers, too.

After they left, while we did the dishes, my mother said, "Annie, you don't have to hide in your room the minute Joe sets foot in the house."

"Hide in my room!" I was indignant. "Maybe you didn't notice there was a kid here needing entertaining. I thought you two might appreciate some privacy."

"Annie, we're not after privacy here." She gave me a rather confused look. "You do like Joe, don't you?"

I hesitated. It wasn't the first time she'd asked. "Well, yeah."

"I thought you did."

"Is that important?"

"Of course it is. Very important."

"Because you're in love with him?"

"That, too. And also because Joe's very decent. He's kind, he's fair – " She smiled at me. "And he's funny."

"His wife didn't think he was so funny."

"I think they were just too young when they married. They weren't prepared for what marriage meant."

"Are you?"

"What?"

"Prepared for what it means?"

"Probably not, I've never been married. Besides – "

I could tell by the way she kept smiling at me that she wanted to keep me reassured that she wasn't about to turn our lives topsy-turvy. But she had admitted being in love. A first. Everything *could* change.

"You know, Annie, I am being cautious – as I'd want you to be before stepping into unknown territory. Both

Joe and I have a child to consider. And things are improving for you and me, albeit slowly. I'm proud of us – especially of you and your scholarship."

"But, Mom, you must think about marrying him."

"Some. But I want to enjoy what Joe and I have right now."

My mother still held that reassuring smile on me. Except it couldn't touch my deepest worry. If she decided to get married, what place would my real father have in my life? Not that he had much of one now. But if Joe came in, my father might disappear from that niche in my head forever.

I couldn't believe I was even having such a thought. I squeezed my eyes shut hard, trying to wish it away.

CHAPTER THREE

WHEN I OPENED MY EYES the next morning my mother was standing over my bed ready to leave for work.

"Annie, I'm sorry to wake you."

"What time is it?"

"Almost eight. You don't have to get out of bed yet. The apartment's freezing."

"No, I want to get up," I said, without moving. "Linda's coming over early."

"If you go out, please dress warmly. I may be a little late because of the Christmas party after work. It won't be much. I shouldn't be too late. You'll find some money on my bureau. But please, Annie, go easy on pizza and junk. This week I'm really short. I had to pay tuition, and the bill from the dentist was almost twice as much as I expected."

I hated it when my mother went on about our

finances, which were always lousy. What made it worse was that one of the families I depended on for baby-sitting jobs had moved away. The others were in practically the same financial state we were. Or like the Deksnises: it had to be an emergency before they'd call me.

It hurt that I couldn't get my mother a really nice Christmas gift instead of the usual cheap cologne or infectious earrings.

I slipped out of bed and got dressed fast. I was shivering. Steam that the super was finally sending up whistled through the radiator pipes. When I reached under the bed for my shoes I saw the box. I dragged it out and brought it into the living room with me where I plopped it down on the sofa to retie it before taking it back to Mrs. Maxstead.

Maybe if I called first I could tell her I wasn't able to wear it because it didn't fit right. And I wanted to drop it off in case she wanted to give it to someone else. That way I could just hand it to Alma at the door, even though I knew Mrs. Maxstead would think I was terribly ungrateful, returning it. So what, she thought I was dirt already. Then I remembered Candy's funeral. Oh well, at least it would be ready to take to her tomorrow.

As I was lifting the jacket out to refold it neatly, a piece of paper stuck to the bottom of the box caught my eye. The price, including the tax, it said, was one hundred sixty-five dollars. And that slip was all you needed for an exchange or refund, within ten days of purchase. According to the date, Mrs. Maxstead had bought it six days ago. That meant you could just walk into Mannerheim's and exchange it for anything in the store. Or get all that money.

I sat there thinking hard about what was printed on the sales slip, although it was perfectly clear exactly what it meant.

I could leave the jacket in the box, and from all the attention it had gotten so far, no one would probably care. Certainly not Bernice, who hadn't shown an ounce of curiosity yesterday. Mrs. Maxstead was close to tears when she pushed the box at me and said, "Just take it out of my sight." She certainly would never want to see it on me.

So, the jacket was truly mine. Therefore it was my right to do exactly what I wanted with it. Including taking it back. For the money.

I sat thinking and staring at a spot in the carpet that was so threadbare it looked like lace. I was trying to make the answer come out right, I mean, to make the jacket and the money equal to each other. As long as the jacket stayed a jacket, it was mine. But once it became money …

After a while I got up from the sofa. I didn't want to think about it anymore. Everything just went in circles. Besides, I hadn't had breakfast or made the beds or anything. But I couldn't stop thinking about it.

A hundred sixty-five dollars was chicken-feed to the Maxsteads. Hell, Bernice spent that much on a casual shopping trip. And she was forever telling me about restaurants where it cost more than the jacket to sip the water. So why should I worry over getting the refund? I was being stupid. That's how rich people got rich – they didn't act dumb about money. My jacket. My money. Tough luck, Mrs. Maxstead.

A little after ten the doorbell rang.

"Annie, it's me," came from the intercom.

Linda has a really deep voice, and boy, is it sexy. I'd flung open the door and was leaning over the banister. She was running up the stairs, and we fell into a hug as soon as she hit the landing.

"Yo!" she said, snapping at the elastic, "you're wearing a bra!"

"The neighbours will be thrilled to hear it. Started just after you left." I pulled her into the apartment.

"Aw, Annie, life was hard enough when you only had a fabulous face. I was hoping you'd stay a little girl forever."

"Gee, thanks a lot." I threw her a mock grin in return, and we both started to laugh.

"So, hey, Lin, do I look any different to you?" I spun around.

"Nope. Just uglier."

"Come on, I'm serious. You know what I mean. Do I look like, well, more ... older? You do."

"No kidding?"

"Honest."

"It's not just the makeup?"

"Uh-uh. But I'm not sure exactly what."

She made a face. "My feet got bigger."

She was wearing her electric blue sneakers. We'd

painted our shoes last winter. Except I'd outgrown mine. "So how come if your feet got bigger you can still wear your Day-Glos?"

"Jeez, Annie, do you have to be so logical? All I'm saying is, if something has to get bigger, why can't it be my boobs?"

"Your boobs are plenty big. You sound like some-one-who-shall-remain-nameless."

Linda squealed. "Aha! The solid-gold whine decanter you're always telling me about on the phone. What's her name?"

"Bernice?"

"Yeah, that's right. I'd like to meet her."

"Bernice? You want to meet Bernice? You've got to be kidding."

"No. She sounds interesting."

"I can't believe this. We're talking ditzoid here."

"I can't help it if you make a wing-nut sound inter-esting. Okay, look, it's no big deal. I don't mean I want to meet her now, this minute. Hey, let's go downtown and check out the Christmas sights, like every year. We can catch up on what's been happening on the way."

"Great. I'll get my things."

"First I have to go to the bathroom," Linda said, yank-ing off her beret, under which she'd tucked all her hair.

"You dyed your hair!" I screamed.

She shook her head like a wet puppy.

"Wow! You really went for it." Linda's hair was brassy blonde and buzzed. Her natural colour is light brown. Just a little darker than mine.

"New town, new woman." She batted her eyes at me.

"Hey, I noticed the false lashes. Trying to start a tornado in here?" The disapproval sneaked out of my voice. "But Lin, your own are so long."

"A little help can't hurt," she said, peeling off her coat.

I stared, amazed at her skin-tight sweater, and jeans that stuck to her crotch and fanny like a magnet was pulling them.

"You don't approve of the new me, Annie." Her tone was edgy.

The Linda of barely six months ago was light years away from this flashy stranger. "I'm just surprised. Remember what you used to call jeans that tight?"

"No. What?" She was irritated and had her hands on her hips.

"Slut butts."

"I must have been ten years old and a first-class dork."

"And you're not supposed to just smear lipstick across your mouth."

I was shocked – but at myself. Here I was giving Linda the same treatment Bernice dished out to me. She flounced into the bathroom. I knew I'd better get it together. I went for my things.

When I came back Linda was examining the box on the sofa.

"Annie, what is this?" she asked, looking over at me.

"Oh, it's a jacket," I said.

"That much I can see. Is it yours?" Her voice was full of surprise. "It's beautiful." She turned the box around. "You bought something in Mannerheim's? You win the lottery?"

"No, I didn't buy it. Someone gave it – " I decided not to tell Linda too much " – to my mother as a gift for me." I took a deep breath. "My mother and I did a number of favours for this person, and she knew my mother wouldn't accept anything for herself."

"No fooling. What did you do?"

"It's a long, boring story. My mother wants me to exchange it. Well, actually get a refund. Do you mind?"

"You mean now?"

"Yes, if I'm going to return it I have to do it today."

"But, Annie, don't you want to keep it? I love the colour."

"Lin, nobody wears anything this dressy at school. It's too pretty. Where do I go that I could ever wear it?"

"Yeah, I see your point. So let's go."

Mannerheim's. The minute Linda and I stepped through the door we started to giggle.

Everything sparkled. The crystal chandeliers, the bottles of cologne and cosmetics, the counters – even the shoppers. Clones of Mrs. Maxstead. Piped-in music filled the air, the sound clear and silvery like the decorations.

"Hey," Linda asked, "how come this is the first time we've been here? You might think we never lived in this city."

"Here's how come," I said, shoving a price tag under her nose.

"A bargoon. Must be on sale." She was going crazy

checking price tags while I dragged around the box.

After I found out where to take the jacket, all the clerk did was read the receipt, remove the jacket from the box and ask if I wanted a credit note or a refund.

"Re-re-" I started, stumbling over the word. "Refund," I said apologetically, with a stiff smile.

She wrote something on the slip and told me to take it up to the credit office.

There another clerk counted out the dollars while my heart pounded in my ears. My cheeks were burning. My jacket, my money, I kept thinking. Until I heard Linda urge, "Come on, Annie," and pull me into the elevator just as the doors were closing.

When we got off at the ground floor I jammed the money in my bag.

"Annie, is anything wrong? You look spooked."

"Spooked?" My laugh sounded phoney even to me.

"This place must be too rich for your blood."

Back on the street Linda was oohing and aahing and dragging me over to look in every store window.

"Oh, Annie, look at this," she squealed.

We watched mannequins on a merry-go-round catching gifts as they passed a Santa Claus. What would the One Who Rules think if she knew she'd become my personal Santa Claus? Probably not her first career choice, considering the way she was always putting me down. And she was always referring to my "parents," knowing perfectly well I only lived with my mother. I may have managed to get the money and the jacket to finally come out equal. But there was no way she would ever let the Langs come out equal to the Maxsteads.

"Annie, know what I'm going to do today? Get Jeffrey a Christmas gift."

"Jeffrey?" I asked vaguely. "Who's Jeffrey?"

Linda hung a drop-dead look on me. "I knew you weren't listening to a single word I said on the subway."

It was true. I tried making a joke of it. "Hey, come on, Linda, you know it's impossible to hear the human voice on the subway. How soon they forget."

"Annie, I know you. When your mind's off somewhere you get this ... this glazed-over look, like a zombie."

"Oh, well, thank you."

"Yeah, well, it's the truth."

We both looked away. It was up to me to apologize. Not that I felt like it. "Look, Lin, I'm sorry. I forgot how ... sensitive you can be."

Linda's eyes flashed. "Don't dump on me, Annie! You're the one who's been positively freaked out since we left that store. It's been going on all morning. You noticed me back at the apartment just enough to look down your nose at my hair and clothes."

"That's a crock, Linda." I managed to sound equally testy. But she was right. It used to be we could tell each other everything. But now, I don't know — I couldn't tell her about the jacket and all. Maybe I was afraid she'd pass moral judgement on me. Or maybe ... well, maybe we'd really lost touch.

I took a stab at fixing things. "Okay, I admit it. I'm sorry. My mind shoved off in another direction. It's kind of – well, I'm hung up on this boy I met, and … "

"Really?" She was trying to act cool, hide her excitement. "Who is it?"

Actually I could use her advice. There was no one else to talk to about Sean. "He's someone I met recently. I like him a lot."

"No kidding, Annie."

I nodded. "We held hands." I must have made it sound like the event of the century. Well, to me it was. Besides, telling her got Linda simmered down.

"I hate the way some guys hold your hand," she said. "They act like they have to *do* something with it. And they keep squeezing like they're kneading dough."

"Sean didn't do that. He's not stuck-up or anything but he just knows things – how to act. Things. He's not like the jerky kids at school used to be. Hey, what do you mean how some guys hold hands?"

"You know, I told you."

"No."

"C'mon, Annie, I told you right after we moved to Bakersville I met this girl and she invited me to a couple of parties."

"Oh, yeah, I remember that. And you said you could tell right off you'd fit in with the kids up there."

"And about the two parties I went to?"

"Okay, but you didn't mention anything about holding hands, Linda. You know darn well I'd remember that."

"Well, maybe I didn't. These guys turned out to be so gross. Anyway, some of us started a new crowd with some other kids. So this – what's his name – Sean is real cool, huh?"

"Oh, yeah. Very cool. And very rich."

"Rich?" She made it sound like a foreign word.

"Uh-huh. I think he's going to ask me out."

"So, hey, what's the problem?" She seemed a bit bewildered.

"Tenth Street." Even more bewildered. "Linda, he lives in this fantastic apartment. They have these rugs on the floor like you see hanging in museums. There were four – count 'em, four – bathrooms." I waited. "Well, what do you think I should do?"

"Simple problem, simple solution. Meet a boy with one bathroom." She stifled a laugh.

"Very funny. Thanks a lot."

"Just trying to keep you from getting dumped later." I made a face. It wasn't what I wanted to hear.

"Hey, Annie, how about lunch?"

"Great. I'm freezing."

"Can we get a burger around here?"

"How about this place?"

Linda looked around. "Where?"

"Right here."

"On the sidewalk? In the parking garage across the street? Annie, we're standing in front of the Samovar."

"I know that," I said brightly.

"I've got four bucks including tip."

"So who asked you? My treat, Linda. Call it a Christmas present." I grabbed her by the arm. "Come on."

She pulled back. "Annie, wait. Listen, I just wouldn't be comfortable in there."

"Why not?"

She shrugged. "I don't know. Would you?"

"The kids from school come here all the time. Not with their parents. By themselves."

"Yeah, so does Mikhail Baryshnikov. I hear he gets a pretty fair allowance."

The brassy bleached hair and tight jeans hadn't changed Linda much after all. "Well, if you'd be that uncomfortable ... "

She looked slightly chagrined. "You really want to do this."

"Well, yeah, I'd sort of like to see what it feels like."

"Don't you have to give that money to your mother?"

"No. Most of it's mine. What do you say? It won't spoil us for burgers to eat in a fancy joint once in our lives."

Her face broke into a broad smile. "Hey, why not. Look where class restaurants got Baryshnikov."

"I bet you need a reservation."

Linda was probably right. I was watching this man who kept looking in a ledger, then ushering people to their tables.

"Let's leave, Annie."

"I'm too cold," I whispered. "Besides, I just got a brilliant idea."

When it was our turn, I said, "We have a reservation. Megan O'Sullivan." His smile told me he recognized the name. I watched him scan the page.

"I don't see it."

"Oh, that's impossible. I can't believe she forgot to call."

"Sorry." He scanned the page once more. "No, it's not here."

I looked over at Linda. "I guess she wasn't able to reach us to let us know she couldn't make it." I turned back to him and tried to look helpless. "We're famished – and freezing."

Maybe he could smell money, because after a few seconds he said, "I think I have something available."

Linda squeezed my arm as we followed along, to be seated against a banquette wall of red leather with our things piled beside us. A warm glow seemed to envelop everything like a silky cocoon.

"So this is life in the fast lane," Linda said.

"Yeah, that's us."

Linda laughed. "Absolutely."

"And I had to practically break your arm to get you in," I teased.

"I know. But – Annie? Thanks."

"Hold off till we taste the food."

"And get the bill."

Linda didn't know that lots of the time I was forcing myself to be daring. Especially with her, or we'd never do anything.

The truth is – well, maybe Annabelle Styles Whittledge would eat in fancy places, shop in expensive stores, plop down big bucks for stuff whenever she felt like it. Maybe she could always be remarkably daring. But with Annie Lang, most of it was an act.

The thought shook me up. I wasn't unhappy with my life. Except something was making me restless …

Joe? Mrs. Maxstead? Corinth?

We were handed menus.

"He looks mean," Linda said, after the waiter walked away.

"Nah," I assured her. "I think he was only trying to place us. Kids from school come here all the time."

Linda shrugged. "Okay, but we better be real sweet to him. So what are you going to have?"

"Get caviar," I joked.

"Yuck," she groaned. "Disgusting."

"When did you ever eat caviar?"

"Last summer at my aunt's wedding."

"I like it," I said.

"You like caviar?"

"Sure. I really pigged out on it last month at Sean's sixteenth birthday party. His sister's in my class, and she invited me."

You could almost see Linda's mind boggling. "A girl in your class served caviar for her sixteenth birthday?"

"No, her brother's birthday."

Linda shook her head. "That's crazy. The only reason my aunt had it is her new husband is a salesman in a fancy delicatessen."

We studied our menus again. "Hey, Annie, what do you think this chicken Kiev tastes like?" She pronounced it Keeve.

"Who knows? Anyway, it's pronounced Kiev, like the city."

"Oh well, if I can't even pronounce it, I'm certainly not eating it."

"Good idea," I agreed. "The hot borscht sounds perfect for today, though. I'm having that. Dessert afterward."

"Yeah, that's what I'll get, too."

"Do you want a Coke, Lin, something to drink?"

"A Coke's fine. Are you having one?"

"Uh-uh, mineral water."

"What?"

"You know."

"You're actually going to pay to drink water? They don't have free water here?" She had that devilish glint in her eye.

My voice sounded out in a singsong. "Come on, Linda, behave."

"Yeah, but I hate the idea of paying for H_2O, even with bubbles in it."

"I'm paying, remember?"

"Right," she said. "Make that two pay waters." We started giggling. I raised my head. The waiter was standing over us looking annoyed. I gave him the order.

The minute he walked away, we began laughing really hard, finally gasping just to catch our breaths. The couple at the next table glanced over and smiled.

"Oooh, Annie. They like us. We're a hit," Linda said, which started us giggling all over again.

It was like old times. I forgot all about Mrs. Maxstead, the jacket, the money, even the posh restaurant.

Our food arrived. Steaming plates of thick dark soup, with sour cream and little meat pies. Then the mineral water was poured. I was afraid Linda would have another giggling kick because of all the attention. But we were both too hungry and went straight for the food as soon as the waiter left.

"Hey, Annie," Linda said, wolfing down the last meat pie before we'd even gotten half through our soup. "Think we can get more of these?"

"Sure, if the waiter ever comes back this way."

Finally, when he stopped by the table next to ours, I signalled him, and Linda gave him her don't-ruffle-his-feathers smile.

"We'd like two more orders of these meat pies, please," I said.

"Piroshki," he snapped. I expected him to click his heels.

I could see Linda's mouth open. Whatever she was planning to say would get us laughing again. I kicked her in the shin. When the waiter walked away, she claimed innocently, "I thought he was introducing himself. Fred Piroshki. I was only going to tell him our names."

"Oh, you're bad," I said.

"God, wait till I tell the kids back home about this," Linda said.

"Who do you hang out with up there?"

"Oh, just regular guys. We dress very tough, but we're not. Looking tough but being fluff."

"Run that by me again?"

"I think there once were some really tough kids in the school, and someone tried to lighten things up by getting everyone to look that way."

I was pretty confused myself. "Everyone tried to look tough," I asked, "even if they weren't?"

"Well, maybe not everyone." Linda looked pretty vague, too. "I'm not really sure what it was all about. It was already going on when I started there. I just followed along. Like, maybe it would help me to fit in? And it did."

She scraped the bottom of the plate for the last bit of borscht. "Take my friend Hillary Berger, for instance. She has her hair dyed the most amazing red. All spiked out and moussed to death. She looks like she spits nails. But raise your voice to this girl, she'll just about burst into tears. We're known throughout the school district as the fluffy toughs."

"Right," I said. Linda had put me on long enough.

"It's true, Annie. You can ask my mother."

"Your mother lets you out of the house looking like a juvenile Hell's Angel?"

Linda began to laugh. "At first she threatened to send me to convent school. But once she started meeting the kids and realizing how harmless they were, she simmered down."

"Just a litter of fluffy kittens." That got me a bop on the head.

"Look, Annie, it's fun. I mean I'd never have the nerve to dye my hair or dress in jeans this tight if everyone wasn't doing it."

For sure. The old Linda thought too-tight sweaters and jeans were what you wore to send out the message you were ready for action.

Still, it was hard for me to picture Linda with a group of punkers.

"Annie." She started to laugh. "My mother calls it the school uniform."

We were close to hysteria when the waiter stared us into submission. Linda forced herself to stop laughing by blowing out her cheeks while trying to put on her syrupy smile. I couldn't look at her.

"Will you young ladies have anything else?" he asked, raising his eyes prayerfully that we wouldn't.

"Yes," I replied in my most ladylike manner. "We'll have dessert."

"I'll bring the menu."

But I'd already seen a display of pastries. "I'll have a pastry," I told him.

My quick decision earned me a "Very good." He turned to Linda. "And you?"

She nodded. She couldn't talk with her face locked into that gruesome position.

"Is that tea in all those tall glasses?" I asked the waiter.

"Yes. You want tea?"

"Uh-huh."

Linda's cheeks started to deflate like balloons.

"That tea looks hot," she said.

"Of course, madame," he said archly.

"At my house, tea in tall glasses like that, it's always iced and – "

I kicked her under the table again. "Two pastries and two teas, please," I said sweetly.

The dishes were cleared from our table. The tea was brought, then the waiter returned with the tray of pastries. You'd think we'd never seen a pastry in our entire lives.

"What's that?" Linda asked, pointing.

"A napoleon." The waiter's stone-cold expression showed he knew he was going to have to identify every cake on the tray.

"And that?"

"Apricot tart."

"What's this one?"

"Baba au rhum."

"Baba whom?"

"It has rum in it, Linda."

She looked at me, wide-eyed. "Honest? Wow. I can get drunk on it. I'll take that."

"And I'll have the napoleon," I told him.

Linda pierced the baba with her fork. "I'm having a terrific time, Annie," she said, and plopped a piece in her mouth.

"No fooling? I never would have guessed." I was having a pretty good time myself.

"Yeah, this will be my best Christmas gift. Outside of four bucks I have in my purse right now, actually three eighty-five, I'm broke. So I won't be able to return the treat."

"I'm crushed."

"Here, have a taste." She fed me a bite. "Tremendous, huh?"

"Yeah, very good," I said, slicing a small square from my napoleon and handing it to her. "You'll like this, too."

"Mmm, delish. Only not as special as my boozy one. Say, I know what. I'll reward you with a picture of Jeffrey." She eyed me with a sidelong glance. "If you ask me who Jeffrey is again – " Her voice threatened. "Can you believe it, Annie? Me. A boyfriend."

"Sure," I said, plunking a sugar cube into my tea. "Every female in creation will have one before I do."

"Very funny." Linda grimaced. "You should have gone after a scholarship to a co-ed school. Then you wouldn't be stuck with a bunch of rich, spoiled, snooty girls." She scraped the last crumbs from the baba into her mouth and pushed the plate aside.

"I never said Corinth girls were snooty. Rich and spoiled, yes. Snooty, heaven forbid. At Corinth, it's just not done to be a snob."

"Oh, sure."

"No, honestly. They're terminally broad-minded. They really think you can't point to them and cry *money*."

"What's the point of being rich if you pretend you're not?"

"Here, finish this." I slid my unfinished napoleon over to her. "Not looking like you're well-off is as important at Corinth Academy as dressing tough is at your school."

"They dress down, huh? Yeah, you've got to be a millionaire for that look." Linda cleared the plate of the napoleon.

"Oh, no," I said broadly. "I have a new style that's even classier than throw-away."

"Than what?" Linda asked, perplexed.

"Throw-away. The Corinth look. I go them one better. Worn-away. Take this, for instance." I picked up my jacket and pointed to the bottoms of the sleeves, where I'd worn the fabric down almost paper thin.

"Now this is an excellent example of worn-away but not throw-away. Which automatically puts it way above anything else." I poked her in the ribs so that she wouldn't start on another laughing jag. "Here he comes again."

Our waiter set a small tray down on the table with the check on it, then walked away.

"What's the damage?" Linda asked. "They never put it face down in the places I go to eat."

"Never mind," I said, leaning out of reach.

"We can wash dishes, Annie."

"Very funny." I got out three ten-dollar bills and a five.

"Between thirty and thirty-five bucks? Just to eat soup for lunch? Of course, the French water jacked the price up. Not to mention the booze in my pastry."

The bill had come to twenty-eight dollars plus the tax. I remembered hearing that you doubled the tax for the tip. So I left all the change, which was four dollars and seventy-six cents. I felt very efficient and grown-up.

As we walked toward the front Linda pulled furiously at my sleeve.

"Annie, those three guys are giving us the eye."

"What three guys?" I spun around to face the door. "Oh, my God."

"You know them?"

I nodded. "The one in the middle is the one I like."

"You mean Mr. Four Bathrooms? They're all gorgeous."

Sean was coming toward us, followed by Josh

Morgenstern and Syd Darby, all dressed in upper-crust casual: heavy sweaters with thick high turtlenecks, classic navy blazers. And trailing practically to the ground, these fantastic long woollen mufflers. Acid-washed jeans, like Mr. Taber's, and hiking boots. Exclusive private school was written all over these guys, and it didn't get by Linda.

"Annie, what a surprise!" Sean beamed.

"Hi, Sean." I said hello to the others and introduced Linda. She responded in her sexiest voice. Josh was already sidling up to her.

"You weren't leaving, were you?" Sean asked.

"Yes, we are," I told him, really pleased he was so clearly disappointed.

"Hey," Syd suggested, "why not join us anyway? You two can afford to eat a little more. Not like me." He patted his ample midriff.

Sean looked from me to Linda. "How about it?"

"Well, much as we'd love to," Linda said, giving the false lashes a real workout, "I for one have to get back to Bakersville."

I was having a hard time keeping a straight face.

"You live in Bakersville?" Josh asked, just as the man who checked reservations came over and told us we were blocking the entrance.

"Why, yes, I do," Linda said brightly, like she was announcing she lived in the penthouse suite of some fancy hotel.

"Let me have your number," Josh said, "I get up to Bakersville once in a while."

"And let me give you mine in the city," Syd offered.

"For when you're back in town again, which I hope will be soon."

"You're cute, Syd." Josh gave him a nasty look.

Sean and I exchanged amused smiles.

"I'll tell you what," Linda suggested coyly. "When you're ready to come to Bakersville, Josh, you can get it from Annie. And next time I expect to be back here, Syd, why, Annie will let you know. But now I do have to leave."

"I wish you didn't, Annie," Sean said to me. "Oh, by the way, we're cooking up a terrific plan for New Year's Day. The same kids who were at my party. In fact I was going to call you tonight about it. Will you be home?"

"I expect to be." I knew darn well I would.

"Great. I'll talk to you then." We all said goodbye, and Linda and I walked out of the cosy warmth and light of the Samovar into the raw, grey, cold air.

The minute we hit the sidewalk, Linda whooped, "I made a conquest."

"Two conquests."

"Rich, too, aren't they?"

I nodded vigorously.

"I wonder what they would have done if my platinum buzz wasn't completely hidden under this beret."

"Or if they'd known you were really a fluffy tough. Just seeing you bat those false eyelashes made their day."

Linda reached up to bop me, but I swung away, into the path of a group of people, one of whom let loose with a string of curse words, ending with "asshole." This set us off laughing again. It had taken us most of the afternoon, but we were back to old times.

"Hey, Annie!" Linda had stopped dead still, causing pedestrian confusion again. "Why are we heading up-town?"

"We're going to Philharmonic Hall." I had sped up my steps, and Linda was hop-skipping to keep up with me.

"What for?"

"I'm going to get my mother and Joe tickets to the opera. She's never been."

"Oh, yeah, she always has opera on the radio."

"You'll have to help me, Lin. I don't know one opera from another."

"Naturally, I do."

"Well, once when Joe was humming something I asked him what it was. I can't remember what he told me, but I think I'd recognize the name if I saw it."

"Your mother's still seeing him?" She sounded mildly surprised.

"Yep."

"Annie, stop walking so fast. I'm not getting a chance to look at anything."

"There are no stores along here, anyway," I said, without changing my pace.

"Boy, you're spending that money like water ... with bubbles."

We were waiting for the light to change. "My mother never had a decent Christmas present in her life," I said, tight-lipped.

Linda glanced over but didn't react. The minute the light flashed green I rushed across the street.

By the time we arrived at Philharmonic Hall, I had it all worked out in my head. Seeing Sean just now helped to give me the idea. Megan's and Sean's mother was an agent for classical performers. Megan was always attending the ballet or symphony or something like that. So it should be easy to convince my mother I'd gotten the tickets from her really cheap. Maybe even free.

I took a program schedule from one of the wall holders in the lobby. Linda leaned over my shoulder, reading it with me.

"We'll need a translator," she wisecracked. "Hey, we'll do it like the menu at the restaurant. If we can't pronounce it we don't buy it."

"There wasn't anything on the menu I couldn't pronounce," I reminded her smugly, with a playful jab.

"Okay, but just try some of these. How about this? Dye Val-cure."

"*Die Walküre* is pronounced Dee Val-kour-ie."

"Oh, yeah? How do you know?"

"Because I heard it pronounced on the radio when my mother was listening. Come on, Linda, help me."

"Is this the one you were trying to think of? *Così Fan Tutte*? Sounds like an ice-cream flavour."

Out loud we stumbled over the foreign names, laughing so hard I was sure I would burst.

"Here it is!" I shouted triumphantly, so that people in the box office line gaped at us. I dropped my voice to a whisper. "*La Bohème*. Let's go."

The seat prices were enough to give me a heart attack. I decided to buy the second cheapest. Maybe my mother would be less suspicious.

The seats would be in the balcony. The tax brought them to almost forty dollars. They were right below a section called the family circle. But they didn't have any available until February, the man behind the cage informed me. How many people can like opera?

Linda had wandered into the gift shop. When I found her, she was holding up a white T-shirt with a pink pirouetting ballerina.

"I'd get this if I had the money," she said, taking a few mincing steps.

"I can let you have some, Lin." It felt good.

"Nah, I can live without it." She put it down. "Besides, think of what it would do to my tough image."

I smiled. Bernice would have bought two.

My eye caught a small shirt that was pale blue with a wooden soldier stamped on it, from *The Nutcracker*. I bought it.

"Who's that for?" Linda asked me.

"Joe's kid."

"Is it that, like, serious between Joe and your mother?"

"I wish I knew."

"Hey, remember when we came here on a tour in fifth grade, Annie?"

"Mrs. Oppenheim's class. And Vincent Standinski got lost."

"Yeah, too bad he ever got found." Linda took my arm and we started for the subway.

With Bernice I always seem to be trailing. We start out side by side, but she'll always end up in front.

With Megan, Stacey, Rosemary and some of the other

girls, we walk every which way in a group. But Linda and I, we always walk arm in arm.

At the entrance to the subway, we just sort of stood staring. Linda had a funny expression on her face, when you can't tell if someone is going to laugh or cry.

"If my mother gets on my case when I call, Annie, I promise I'll write."

"Me, too. When'll you be coming back?"

"Easter, maybe. I'm not sure."

"Hey, you have two guys waiting for you," I teased.

She laughed and we hugged goodbye. I waved her down the steps, then crossed the street to go home.

CHAPTER FOUR

AS SOON AS I GOT INSIDE the apartment I hid the Christmas presents. Then I started to get things ready for dinner.

But when the phone rang and I answered to Bernice's voice, my insides turned upside down. I thought I'd resolved everything about the jacket, but obviously I hadn't. I felt kind of sick, ashamed, angry. Oh, hell, I don't know. But then Bernice brought me back to earth with a thud.

No hello, just, "Where have you been all day, Annie?"

"What?"

"I've been trying to reach you for hours. It's after four o'clock."

"I thought the funeral was today."

"It was. Early this morning. I've been home all afternoon. Where were you?"

"How was the funeral?"

"How was it? Jesus, Annie, how would you expect a funeral to be?"

I didn't bother answering. I'd only asked out of politeness, not to hear a gory description.

"Annie." Bernice's voice switched to its familiar whine. "Come on over. I feel rotten. Every time one of my relatives looks at me they either start bawling or pull me into these bone-crushing hugs. I can't take it any more."

Poor Bernice. Deep down she was so helpless. But I wasn't sure I could cope with a house full of Maxsteads, either. "Why not come over here?"

There was a pause. "Hang on a sec."

Bernice had never asked about the jacket. Not one bit of curiosity. Zero. It was really bugging me.

She was back on the phone. "My mother hit the ceiling. No way."

"You should have asked your father."

"What for? He always does whatever she tells him to. So where were you all day, Annie?"

"A friend of mine was visiting from Bakersville. We went uptown. Bernice, I really have to hang up now."

"Oh, all right," she whined.

"We'll get together one day next week. Okay?"

"Fine." I could see her pouting. She hung up with a bang.

After dinner I was on the sofa, reading, when my mother came out of her room ready to meet Joe for a movie. It always startled me to see how young she

90

looked. And every time I thought about it – every time – I'd start fantasizing.

The scene changed, but wherever we were my father would mysteriously appear and catch a glimpse of her. He would fall madly in love with her on sight. He would find out her true identity and discover that I was his long-lost daughter. He'd sweep us up into his fabulous life. Sometimes I'd have us all living in the penthouse of a building like Sean's and Megan's.

It would be a summer evening. All the furniture would be white wicker. My mother would be wearing a white tennis outfit, her hair tied back with a white scarf. I'd be in white shorts with a gorgeous white top. My father, tall and elegant, would be coming home from the office, dressed in a white suit. We'd sit around sipping cool drinks from tall glasses. Dumb, huh?

I'd die before I'd ever admit to anyone I let my mind wander like that. Except I bet the other kids did it, too.

Bernice probably dreamed about some perfect guy falling madly in love with her the minute she got her nose fixed.

But what about Megan, who was cute, bright and had everything? Did she have fantasies, too? Did having everything rob you of dreams? I'd never thought about things that way before.

"You look pretty."

"Why thank you, Annabelle." My mother smiled wistfully. "Will you be all right while I'm out?"

"Sure. Aren't I always?"

"What'll you do?" Before I could answer she said, "Maybe next month we'll get the TV fixed. Even I miss it," she said, and laughed. My mother watched television about twice a decade. "So what do you plan to do?"

"I think I'll finish all my homework. Then I'll be free for the rest of the holidays."

"Now that's a sensible idea," she said, blowing me a goodbye kiss.

Her date with Joe made me think of the opera tickets. I was so glad I bought them. It made me feel pretty good about keeping the jacket money. Hey, my jacket, my money, remember?

There was a faint knock on the door. "Who's there?"

"Annie, it's Helen Deksnis."

"Hi, come in."

"No, thanks, Annie, I just stopped by to pay you." She handed me the six dollars. "I'm terribly sorry you had to wait so long. But things haven't been too good recently, and money's really been tight."

I knew more than I cared to about that. "Hey, it's okay," I said.

"We do have a couple of strong possibilities for the New Year. Nick auditioned for a show that's slated to go on the road. And I have a possible – " she crossed her fingers " – reading for a soap. So I may be needing you again."

"Terrific. Hope it works out for you."

"Well, Merry Christmas, Annie."

"You, too, Mrs. Deksnis."

I went back inside and started on my homework. I must have been at it for about an hour when I dozed off, my head on my arms. A doorbell sounded.

Sean, Josh and Syd were standing outside in the hall.

"Instead of calling we decided to come over," Sean was saying.

I just stood there with my mouth open.

"Hey, Annie, what a dump. What are you doing in a hole like this?" Syd asked.

"Yeah," Josh said, "the hall smells like something died out there." They all started to laugh.

"Aren't you going to ask us in, Annie?" Sean asked.

"Forget it, Sean," Josh said. "Let's go before I puke."

"Yeah, enough already," Syd urged.

But Sean just stood staring at me while the other two went banging down the stairs, laughing hysterically.

There was another ring. This one jolted me awake. My arm had fallen asleep, and I felt all cramped and groggy.

"Huh?"

"Hello?"

I recognized Sean's voice immediately. I flicked on the kitchen light. My own hello croaked out.

"Your voice sounds froggy, Annie. Catch cold?"

"Uh-uh." I turned my head away from the mouthpiece to clear my throat. "I dozed off doing homework."

"Homework! No way. Oh, I forgot. You're a brain. Scholarship. Right? Megan told me."

"Guilty." I sighed, trying to sound bored. Oh, hell, I felt so self-conscious. I just didn't know how to act around him.

I tried gazing out the window. Tenth Street seemed drearier than usual. A stray dog knocked over a garbage pail, and a quick wind lifted the papers and whirled them up the sidewalk. A passing car lit up a wino asleep over a cellar grate.

"Beauty, brains and what else?" Sean was asking.

"Huh?"

"Come on, Annie, help me out. Beauty, brains and the third B is – uh-oh, not bisexual, I hope," he kidded.

I was glad he couldn't see me. I was a fourteen-year-old infant when it came to boys. Not that I was the only one with zero experience. Except you'd never know from the way some of the girls talked. The biggest talkers were usually the biggest liars. As for the others, who knows? I'm positive Linda and I will tell each other – if it ever happens.

I'm not sure about Bernice, though. She might shoot off her mouth just to get noticed. First off she'd tell her sister, Joan, the star in the family, to prove she's not just the homely little sister. Joan's already had things fixed – her nose and something with her lips to make them fuller and more sensuous.

All I know is that Sean is the first boy whose attention I like. All I wish is that I didn't get so paralyzed over even the smallest move.

"Breathtaking," he said.

"Blue-blooded," I said.

"Of course, what else. Beauty, brains, and blue-blooded. A thousand pardons, Your Highness."

I managed a small self-conscious laugh. Try bumbling, blushing and bland.

"Annie, I'm sorry you couldn't stick around at the Samovar. We went to see this idiotic movie afterward.

Amphibian Beasts Who Roam the Mummies' Tombs.
We laughed so hard the usher came over and threatened to throw us out." Sean chuckled. "Then he did."

"Really?"

"Yeah, we couldn't stop. And Josh, well, you know, he has this real wicked laugh, like an orangutan's mating call. Maybe your civilizing influence would have saved us."

"Oh, for sure," I said. I couldn't come up with anything else. Luckily Sean was better at this than I was.

"You should have heard Syd after you left. He kept going on about Linda, I'm in love! Linda, I love you! Linda, come back! Marry me, Linda! He was really getting Josh pissed off."

Silence.

"Annie, I want to tell you about this idea we cooked up. We thought we'd get together the kids who were at my party and go up to this ski lodge that belongs to Josh's parents. They're down in the Bahamas, and he has the key."

"Sean, I – I don't know how to ski."

"No problem. There's hardly ever enough snow up there anyways. It's strictly an investment. Building's just about to boom up there."

"Oh."

"But this lodge has an enormous fireplace, great food, sauna – everything you need. Anyway, my parents said Megan and I can go. New Year's Day. After I get back."

"Get back?"

"We're going to Mustique for the holidays. But my parents have to attend this ball on New Year's Eve, and we'll be returning the day before. Everybody thinks it's a terrific idea. How about it?"

"Uh-huh. Sounds great."

"Honest? You don't sound too enthusiastic, Annie."

"Well, it's just that I'll have to get permission, Sean."

"Oh, sure, I understand. Everyone else has to, too. But the idea's ace, don't you agree?"

"Absolutely." I meant it, too. "How far is it from here, Sean?"

"A little over a hundred miles. Less than two hours, if the traffic's good. Oh, that's another thing. We're going to try to get a ride up. So you can tell your parents – "

Parents. That word again.

" – and it's the truth, we're hoping to get rides. Josh's sister and Stacey Wasserman's brother have their own cars. So we're asking them along. Anyway, in a pinch we can always hop a train."

"Isn't it kind of expensive?"

"With all of us chipping in for gas and tolls, it won't amount to anything. Regardless, we go. What the hell."

"Sure, what the hell." Just as well he couldn't see my mocking expression. Don't get me wrong. I really did want to go. Not just to be with Sean. I missed hanging out with a bunch of kids having fun. What if it took money? Big deal. I had the cash, so why not? Just once.

"I'll call you the minute I get back with how we'll be going and everything."

There was a pause. As if he didn't want to hang up quite yet. I still couldn't think of anything to say.

"You headed out of the city, Annie? Someplace warm and sultry? Mustique, maybe?"

"Uh-uh."

He laughed. "I'll plan it better next time. Well, I'll talk to you when I get back, okay?"

"Sure."

"S'long, Annie."

"Bye, Sean."

Now, how would I get my mother to agree?

Christmas went pretty much like the rest of our lives. My mother and I were alone for most of the day. Joe would be coming over in the evening.

I hardly did anything with a group of kids anymore. And lately, outside of school, I didn't seem to be doing much of anything at all. I think that's partly why I was so anxious to go to the ski lodge.

I decided the best way to get my mother to say yes was not to ask too soon. That way she wouldn't have too much time to change her mind. If I asked her the day before, even if she said no, I'd have a whole day to work on her.

When Joe came by we exchanged Christmas gifts. Mine was a knockout sweater, hand-knit and fabulous. Mainly it was dark blue, but it had a free-form design in these off-shade colours, muted and subtle. Eggplant, the deepest red of autumn leaves. It had just the right amount of bagginess.

"Hey, Joe," I said, holding it up against me, "I bet your aunt made this."

"Nope, made it myself between fares." He was grinning from ear to ear.

Joe lived over his aunt's grocery store. I'd seen sweaters she'd made on Joe and Mathew and would have loved to have the nerve to ask her to make one for me.

"Try it on, Annabelle, so we can report back how it looks on you."

I danced into my mother's room where there's a longer mirror than mine. I had to admit it. It looked terrific. "Look, Mom, she got it just perfect." I turned to Joe. "How did she know to get it just right?"

"Oh, she and Betts were in a great conspiracy over it. And she has granddaughters your age. She knows what kids like. Here, Annie," he said, taking a small package from his pocket. "I can't take credit for Aunt Stella's work. This is from me."

I tore the wrappings from the small box. "Oh, Joe." I laughed happily. "You got it perfect, too." I kissed him. It was one of those oversized gag watches lots of the girls wore. "Okay, open mine now."

Joe picked it up from the table. I had put it at the base of the poinsettia plant we'd gotten for decoration. There was another small envelope there, too, for me from my mother. That had me curious.

"It says for Bettina and Joseph." He turned to my mother. "You open it, Betts."

I had folded a small piece of gold foil paper over the envelope. She slipped it off and pulled out the tickets. Her mouth dropped open.

"Annie." Her voice dropped, too. "My God, Annie." Her face froze in that shocked expression.

"What is it?" Joe asked, shifting his gaze from her to me. "Let me see, Betts."

She extended her arm without moving her eyes from

my face. Joe took the tickets from her outstretched hand. A wisp of a smile curled around my mother's mouth. Then it burst free like kids busting out of school. She drew me into her arms.

Joe yelled, "Yippee! We're going to the opera!" He pulled me from my mother's hold. "My turn," he demanded, giving me a big bear hug.

When he let me go my mother's voice was hesitant, confused. "But, Annie, how in the world could you buy these?"

The lie was well prepared. I had even practised my delivery. "Oh, Mom, don't pay attention to the price on the tickets."

I looked from my mother to Joe with a little feeble shrug. Their sympathetic, loving glances were making my throat close from guilt.

"You know, Megan O'Sullivan's mother is a concert agent and – "

"Oh, I didn't know that," my mother interrupted, but suddenly seemed only mildly interested in my story. She and Joe were standing real close. He had one hand on her neck and was rubbing it. Nice. I thought I'd like someone, maybe Sean, to do that to me.

"Anyway, Megan said her mother couldn't use them. I got them way discounted."

"They're terrific, Annie," Joe said.

"I was afraid you had skimped on lunches. I didn't know what to think," my mother said, still flustered. But then she laughed, and my heart turned over with contentment.

"We are going to hear La Bohème," Joe sang out.

"Dinner first, monsieur?" she asked.

"Certainly not, madame. Supper afterward."

"Ah, yes, of course. I'll wear my tiara."

"And I, white tie and tails." They started dancing around the room to Joe's humming.

I turned the radio on, looking for something appropriate. All Christmas carols — not a thing for dancing. We'd have to settle for "White Christmas."

Watching them glide around our tiny, crowded living room, I realized I rarely saw them together. At least not this way. Usually they'd just be sitting across our kitchen table, talking. With me somewhere around the apartment.

Another thing, I never had any fantasies about my mother and Joe. When she was in my daydreams it was with my father. He was the hero. He'd be the one dancing with her or being amusing and charming. It was like I was seeing them for the first time. Seeing … well, something I'd never let myself see before.

"White Christmas" faded, and they stopped. I applauded. "Mom, I didn't know you could dance that well."

"I can't. Joe makes me look good even when I'm stepping on his toes."

"Hey, Betts, the tickets are for February fourteenth."

"Oh," I apologized. "Those are the only ones Megan's mother had."

He winked at my mother. "Do you think Annie is trying to tell us something?"

She answered with a kiss. It was only on his cheek, but so intimate I looked away.

Before Joe, she used to give me these intense lectures on sex. You couldn't call them discussions, they were too one-sided. From wet dreams to AIDS, she dispensed more info than a newspaper box.

She wasn't telling me stuff I didn't already know. And she knew it. But my mother was worried. Scared I'd become a statistic: teenaged and pregnant. Because she knew all about being infinitely stupid. Like, you know, trusting some boy not capable of handling responsibility. Like my father.

Since Joe appeared she still lectures, but now it's all about feelings, love. She tries to get across the point that being friends – knowing a guy's true character before you commit yourself – is what counts.

Yet when I'm with kids, the main thing is whether some guy is a great hunk or a major dork. And who tried what and how far they got seem to be all that matters.

We exchanged the rest of the Christmas presents. A gift certificate for twenty dollars was in the other small envelope, from my mother to me. Which seemed to prove, what with the jacket money and Mrs. Deksnis having paid me, that money finds its way to those who have money.

Mathew had made me a felt bookmark, and I gave Joe the T-shirt for him. Then I went into my room so they could be alone and exchange their gifts.

After Joe left, my mother was really in a mellow mood. I considered bringing up the subject of New Year's Day. But I was afraid she'd think I was trying to sabotage her day. It was best to wait.

CHAPTER FIVE

THE MINUTE I WOKE UP I knew something was different about the day. Mild and sunny. You could tell without even being outdoors, just watching people on the street. When it's cold people seem to walk with their necks hunched down into their collars like turtles. But the minute it's warm heads pop up like tulips.

After I finished doing the chores around the apartment I was anxious to get out and do something. Only not alone. I started off by calling Stacey Wasserman, then Rosemary Heffington. And I even called Letitia Taylor, and we're hardly that friendly. Their maids or answering machines said they weren't home.

I wasn't in the mood to read but went into my room for a book to keep me going until I could come up with an idea. I glanced at the picture hanging over my desk. A snapshot of me with Millicent Poole, Debbie

102

Feinstein and Carol Breiner, taken on the last day of public school.

We have our arms wrapped around one another and we're grinning from ear to ear. But Linda is missing – she moved to Bakersville a week before school closed.

Corinth was making me forget that I still had some good old friends. We were just all scattered, in different places. Millicent had taken the exam for Corinth, too, and tried for a full scholarship, but didn't make it. But she did win one with a school connected to the university.

Carol is just at a regular high school. And Debbie goes way out – practically to the suburbs – to a school that has a rep for its orchestra and music courses. We figure she'll be a famous violinist one day.

I decided to make up New Year's Day cards with a corny message, like, The Old Year Is Gone. Must Old Friends Be, Too? Let's Get Together. I rummaged through my desk to see what materials I had, then I made a list of what I still needed.

I went into the kitchen to call Bernice. Now that I had money to spend she could tag along, for once, while I went shopping. Then it hit me whose money I was actually going to be spending and I thought maybe asking Bernice wasn't such a good idea. I told myself the jacket was a dead issue with the Maxsteads, but it didn't matter anyway. Bernice said she couldn't come.

"Why not?"

"Because we're expecting a store delivery and someone has to be here."

"Where's Alma?"

"My mother gave her extra days off for Christmas."

"Well, let the doorman take it." I was really annoyed.

"Hardly. It's not just a package, it's furniture, and my mother doesn't want anyone let into the apartment if no one's here."

Even when I tried I couldn't sound as snotty as she did. "Okay," I said, "forget it." Then I noticed the magazine on the kitchen chair, the one with the picture that had reminded my mother of Bernice.

"Too bad you can't come over here. There's something really nice I want to show you."

"Oh, yeah? What is it?"

Good. I had her curious. "Sorry, it's too hard to explain. You have to see it."

"Well, bring it over here. I was going to ask you over, anyway. I want you to see the dress I'm wearing for my date with Jimmy."

Even if I didn't stay long Bernice might mention to her mother I'd stopped over. That was good. It would keep Mrs. Maxstead from suspecting that I didn't want to go over there any more.

"I can't stay long."

"Well, the delivery may come by the time you get here, and then I'll be able to go out with you. What are you shopping for?"

"Just some craft stuff. Oh, all right, I'll come over."

"Now," she ordered. "And don't forget to bring whatever it is you want to show me."

The minute she hung up I had doubts. Still, Mrs. Maxstead wasn't home, and all I really wanted was some time before I had to face her. Maybe till spring, when jackets would be forgotten. Maybe forever.

"Annie, that sweater is fabulous," Bernice said, almost before I had my jacket off.

"Thanks." I beamed. "Christmas present."

"We didn't have any kind of Christmas around here," she said, glumly. "Is that what you want to show me?" She pointed to the magazine. I nodded.

"Okay, let's go in the kitchen. I'm having a Coke. Want one?"

"Sure."

Their kitchen was freshly painted, the tiles sparkling white. There wasn't anything new in it, though. The copper pots, the marble counter tops for chopping food, the cabinets were all the same. Except everything looked brighter. The same thing when they had their living room done over last month. The rugs, upholstery – everything looked like new, but they were the same.

At our place nothing gets redone. Stuff wears out and gets replaced. Like my old mattress that felt like I was sleeping on a bed of rocks, before we could get a new one.

My mother says that things of quality last. Not like junky furniture that just falls apart. Quality's a bargain in the long run, she said, if you can afford it.

"So what's in there you want to show me?" Bernice asked, bringing two Cokes over to the table.

I skimmed through the magazine and turned the picture for Bernice to see. After a while she raised her head and gave me this quizzical look.

"Why are you showing this to me?"

"Look at it hard," I said.

After a few seconds she asked thoughtfully, "You think I look like that?"

"No, not now. But it's how you could look. My mother saw it and thought of you."

Bernice stared at the photo. "Look at that nose. And whadda ya know, even her mouth is as big as mine. Who is she?"

"Some lady who knows everybody. Raises money for worthy causes, that kind of stuff."

She got up. "Want some macadamia nuts?"

"No. All I want to say, Bernice, is that here's a lady who doesn't confuse looks with pretty."

"Me, confused? No way, Annie. Even with a nose job I'm not going to be pretty. But I will have a nicer nose. And another thing. I also don't confuse myself with people like that," she said, poking the picture. "Hey, she probably never once thought she was ugly. She was probably never once told she was ugly. And, for sure, she didn't have my mother. If my mother wasn't forever trying to renovate me, like her damn living room, I might be able to brazen it out like that lady. But no, my mother will never even stand for my not getting my nose fixed. Nose jobs are the minimum required procedure in our family. She's had two."

Bernice stared, daring me to be shocked. I wasn't.

"She acts like we're all big slabs of marble. If we get hacked away and reshapen enough, we'll end up masterpieces. Ah, what the hell. Who cares." She glanced

106

at the picture again. "Interesting. Very interesting." She closed the magazine and held it out to me.

"That's okay. My mother's read it."

"Thanks. Say, Annie. You sure don't take after your mother. Do you look like your father?"

That threw me. I picked imaginary lint from my sweater to avoid Bernice's eye.

"So? Do you look like your dad?"

"Some people think so."

"You know, Annie, you've never once mentioned your father."

"So? What's the big deal?"

"Touchy, touchy," Bernice said, with a victorious smile. Obviously she was over her outburst. "Your parents are divorced, right? So, where does he live?"

"He, uh, moves around a lot."

"He's in the army! The navy! The marines! He's a lost astronaut on some distant planet in outer space!" She had to make sure she had me pissed off.

"I'll tell you about him some other time," I lied. "Right now, cut it out."

"No sweat. Come into my room. I want to show you what I'm wearing tomorrow night."

"How come your mother finally let you go out?"

"I told her I'm becoming an old maid."

"And that did it? Bernice, nobody says that anymore. No one even thinks it."

"Oh, no? My mother does. It's part of her large vocabulary of out-of-date ideas. If you don't go to the Right School, you won't meet the Right Kids – meaning ones with money. If you don't get your nose fixed you'll look Ethnic – meaning Jewish."

"But you're not Jewish."

"My grandmother on my mother's side is half Jewish. That's not the point. Ethnic is out."

"Bernice, I'm going out New Year's." I hadn't meant to say it. It just slipped out.

Bernice looked stunned. "You're going out New Year's Eve?"

"No. On New Year's Day."

Her voice dropped. "New Year's Day. So, going out like you have a date? Or just going someplace?"

"Going out like a date."

"Who with?" The mere idea was too much for her.

"With Sean O'Sullivan and some other kids."

"Oh." She sounded relieved. "You're just going to be with a group."

"Yeah, but Sean asked me."

"So who's Sean? And, come on, Annie. It's not the same as being alone with one guy."

"We'll manage when we get there."

"Where?"

"Up to this ski lodge that belongs to the parents of one of the guys."

"You ... ski?"

Bernice sounded so disbelieving, if I'd let myself I'd have felt worthless.

"Do you have a skiing parka?"

Guilt jabbed me like a hot poker. "What?"

"A skiing parka, Annie. Stop acting dense."

If she thought I was acting dense, she had to know

about the jacket. I had to open my stupid mouth and tell her about the trip. I didn't answer – I felt it was safer to wait to hear what she'd come up with next. I guess she'd ask what the jacket her mother'd gotten for Candy was like. But she didn't.

"Because if you don't – "

I couldn't take much more of this. I was about to have a heart attack, for sure.

" – I have two. I have a new one that's a funky acid green. Great colour. It cost over three hundred bucks. Then I have a ski jump suit." She laughed. "It's a wild pattern, like graffiti. I can lend you that one. And skis. Do you have skis?"

I hadn't asked her. Why was she making these offers? "We're not going up to ski. Just to use the cabin."

"Uh-oh, be careful, Annie," she said, with a nasty tease. "So how did you meet this guy?"

"His sister Megan's in my class. Long red hair. About five feet four."

Bernice shook her head. "Nope. Don't know her. Come on, I want to show you my dress." In her room she reached into the closet and held up a hanger. "Awesome, huh?"

"Fabulous."

"Joan has these long silver earrings she's letting me wear. Wait, I want to show you the shoes."

As she rummaged in the bottom of the closet, a door slammed. "Joan?" Bernice called.

"No, darling. It's Mother."

I was so shocked I blurted out, "I thought your

mother was working today."

Bernice gave me this puzzled look. "She was." Mrs. Maxstead was standing in the doorway. "Is anything wrong?"

"Of course not, dear," she answered, capped teeth shining. "One of our clients came in from Texas. We're taking her out to dinner. I want to change."

"What about Dad?"

"He'll be home shortly. Hello, Annabelle."

All that came out of my throat was a grunt. So I just smiled sweetly and listened to my heart thump.

"I see they haven't delivered the lamps yet. Oh, well, I'll be in the shower, Bernice. Has the mail come?"

"On the desk in the dining room."

"What does it take to get one little thing right? Why isn't it on the hall table?"

Bernice shrugged. "I think Joan put it on the desk."

"And where is Joan?"

"She went somewhere with Teddy Blaker."

"Him?" One word from the One Who Rules and Teddy Whoever was dead meat. I turned to go.

"No, wait, Annie, I didn't show you my shoes yet. Besides, we can do your shopping as soon as my mother gets out of the shower."

"Uh-uh, Bernice. I just remembered something. Gotta go."

But Mrs. Maxstead had turned back and caught us in the doorway.

Before Mrs. Maxstead uttered even one word, I knew. I could see exactly what was going to happen.

"Annabelle," she said. "I know this is rather unexpected, but I would like you to bring back the jacket." I knew I hadn't blacked out because the perfect smile was blinding me. "I had meant to give you a call," Mrs. Maxstead was saying. "But with the suddenness of Candy's death and the funeral, well, I'm afraid I must have become rattled."

Mrs. Maxstead had never been rattled in her life. That friendly smile she had stuck on her face was a lie, too.

I started to speak, but the words sounded like they were coming from somewhere else in the room.

"If you would return it later today or tomorrow I would appreciate it, Annabelle."

The perspiration was pouring out of me. But if it killed me, I wasn't going to be bulldozed by her.

"I'm sorry, Mrs. Maxstead, I don't have the jacket."

There was a well-timed pause. "Excuse me?" She was glaring, but her smile was still set.

"I don't have the jacket anymore."

"I'm having a problem understanding you, Annabelle. What do you mean you don't have it?" She could really hang on to a smile.

"I couldn't wear it. It didn't fit right. But a friend of mine was visiting, and it looked great on her. So I gave it to her." I allowed myself the tiniest of smiles. "You said you never wanted to see it again."

"Well!" The word came out with such force it made Bernice jump. I stayed statue still.

"You are mistaken, young lady! Or perhaps you misinterpreted my meaning. If you couldn't wear it, the only decent thing to do would have been to return it to me."

"I'm sorry, Mrs. Maxstead, I had the impression it upset you."

"And the box? Did you dispose of that as well?" Mrs. Maxstead's smile slipped into a sneer.

"I threw it away. You wanted the box?" I made my-self sound surprised and glanced over at Bernice. All my fear was on her face.

"I don't suppose," Mrs. Maxstead said, the sarcasm raining down, "you happened to notice the sales slip before you threw it away."

If she had yelled *thief* at the top of her lungs, it couldn't have been more plain. My throat felt locked. So I just shook my head.

Whatever she did now didn't matter much. She could tell my mother or make us pay the money back. Maybe she even planned it: give the waif the jacket. Leave the slip in the box. She's sure to steal the refund. The One Who Rules had finally trapped me.

She had been holding her keys, but they dropped to the floor. As she stooped to pick them up, her face lift fell forward and creased into folds like the pleats in a skirt. When she straightened up it smoothed out again. It was very weird. With all the stuff she'd done to her-self she should have been really beautiful. She was okay. But nothing special. And for that she gave Bernice such a crappy time? What a bitch.

She was glaring at me. "Threw it away? That slip was worth almost two hundred dollars on an exchange. Do you think anyone hands *me* two hundred dollars? Do you know what it means to *earn* it?" Her eyes held me with an icy stare. "Such cavalier behaviour, Annabelle. You've shocked me."

I hadn't moved a muscle, hoping it hid how scared I still was. "I never dreamed you wanted it back, Mrs. Maxstead. I'll get in touch with my friend," I bluffed. "Only it may take a while. She's away for Christmas vacation. But – "

"Please, Annabelle – " she cut into my words " – don't play me for a fool. Bernice, you will help me the rest of this afternoon. I'm sure Annabelle will understand." She turned on her heel and left the room, bracelets clanging.

I understood all right. I would never again be welcome in this house.

Why was I fighting back tears? This wasn't Linda or Megan or one of my other friends I was losing. This was only … only Bernice. I always thought I didn't really care about Bernice, one way or the other.

She was still standing awkwardly. "What kind of a jacket was it, Annie? I didn't see it."

"A sort of après-ski jacket. I couldn't wear it and didn't think it would matter to your mother if I passed it on to someone else."

"Is that the same friend from Bakersville you mentioned the other day?"

"Yeah, Linda. I'm going now, Bernice." She nodded and got my jacket. Then there was nothing more to say.

CHAPTER SIX

I LEARNED SOMETHING. You don't necessarily suffocate to death if you can't breathe. My throat was closed, choking on Mrs. Maxstead's words, stuck there. But my legs kept moving, so I had to be alive. Nobody had ever hated me before. Well, fine – it works both ways.

She was the liar ... the cheat. The phoney who gave money to worthwhile causes, as long as she got her name plastered all over it – like the new school wing Corinth was planning to build. Mrs. Maxstead, public benefactor, couldn't bear to let a few measly dollars get away from her.

Okay, so even if she'd honestly forgotten about the sales slip being in the box, and then remembered, she could have let it pass. What difference would it make to her? But oh no, it was confronting me. That's what turned her crank. I slowed down to help me think, to figure it out. Why did she hate me so much?

Maybe poor people scared her. Like we were a dis-
ease you'd catch if you hung around with us. Maybe
deep down she knew some things couldn't be bought
or changed – even with money. Just like, under the
face lifts and nose jobs, her real self was still there, and
she couldn't stand it. And maybe she hated me because
she knew I could stand myself – although she'd think I
had little reason to be pleased with what life handed
me.

There was no other girl at Corinth, no one among
Bernice's friends she'd have dared offer the jacket to.
Only poor, underprivileged Annie Lang. I did her a
favour. I let her dump her charity on me.

But then I outsmarted her. I turned her charity into
power. Money!

The sun was fading, and as usual I was feeling cold. I
speeded up, with new thoughts sneaking into my head.
Worrisome ones. Like how come I'd gotten so greedy?
I wasn't even a bit that way before. Now, when it was
too late, I let myself search for clues, try to understand.
Why? Why hadn't I just taken the stupid jacket back to
Mrs. Maxstead? If you couldn't trust yourself to be honest, who could you trust? Anyone? My mother. There.
She never lied. But she didn't always tell me the whole
truth, did she? Was she being completely honest with
me about Joe? About my father?

These thoughts were getting me really depressed. I
let my mind drift to Candy and all the relatives mourn-
ing her. If I died on the spot, the only person to mourn
me would be my mother. That just made me feel worse,

like I'd lost something I never even had. I couldn't get rid of these gruesome thoughts, so I began to run. Like I could escape from all the stuff I didn't want to think about.

It helped, too. Soon Corinth – and who were really my friends, and honesty, and even Mrs. Maxstead – began to fade. By the time I was too winded to go on I found myself in Little Italy.

I walked along the streets, glancing in shop windows and at the houses, and in the middle of a block, there it was: a sign that said Zucca's Grocery. There were two men and a woman behind the counter serving the customers. I had thanked Joe's aunt on the phone for my beautiful sweater. Her voice fit the smiling, pleasant-looking lady I was watching. She had to be Joe's aunt. I could go in and show her how the sweater looked. But the store was busy. Besides, I wasn't in the mood.

The second storey above the grocery had its own side entrance. I bet plenty of times when my mother told me she and Joe were going to a movie or out somewhere, they were really coming here. In an emergency I was to call Joe's aunt, who could always reach him, my mother told me. So if I got hit by a truck, Joe's aunt would get the news because my mother was doing it, up there, with Joe. Terrific.

Looking up at the windows was making me feel like a pervert. Then I realized that the cars were driving with their lights on. I rushed for the nearest subway.

I had to squeeze in because it was jammed with people leaving work. I prayed my mother wouldn't be home before I got there. But she was.

"I'm home, Mom," I called, sweet as anything.

My mother stepped from the kitchen, a big stirring fork in her hand. She lit right into me. "You're late, Annie."

"I'm sorry."

"That doesn't help."

"Can't I be late once in a blue moon?"

"Not if you don't let me know."

I kind of thought she looked at me funny. Sometimes I get the impression she can tell how I'm really feeling. I mean even when I put on a phoney act. Anyway, she calmed down pretty quick. Just as well: I wanted to keep on good terms until I could tell her about the ski lodge.

"All right, just hurry and get ready for dinner. I'm meeting Joe right afterward."

Oh, so that was it. Just a precious date with Joe. Fine. So maybe what happened with Mrs. Maxstead was a break. If she had called my mother, I'd be dead meat. But if she hadn't done it by now she wasn't going to. The jacket issue was finished. Now I could relax and concentrate on the trip. I still had plenty of dough left. I'd make it stretch. Use it for hanging out at expensive places. I'm a Corinth girl, right.

When I got up the morning of New Year's Eve, the first thought that rushed through my head was that Sean would call. I got the jacket money out from under my mattress and laid it out on the bed. I thought there'd be more. I didn't realize I'd spent close to a hundred dollars. Oh, well, there would still be enough, even if we went by train. And if we were lucky we'd get a ride.

"Breakfast, Annie!" my mother called. "Please hurry."

It was clear as a big soap bubble she was in a terrific mood. "Annie, I'm going to a party tonight."

"You are? No kidding."

"It's at a cousin of Joe's. Will you be okay? I might be late getting home."

"I'll be fine, but isn't this gold-mine night for cab drivers?"

"Joe sold his share of the cab. He's starting work as an accountant on the fifteenth. For the first time in his life he'll have a little nest egg."

Well, if she was feeling that mellow, this was the perfect time to bring up the ski trip – right before she had to leave for work – she'd have to come up with a quick answer, and in her good mood it should be yes.

"Well, Mom, of course I won't be going out tonight to celebrate New Year's Eve with my boyfriend, but – "

She cut in. "Don't worry, sweetie, in time enough you will be."

"No, what I was going to tell you is that I may not be going out tonight, but I have a fantastic invitation for tomorrow."

"Oh, that's nice," she said, jumping up to get the jam – which was right on the table in front of her.

"Mom, will you please sit still a minute." I tried to make my pitch sound very plausible. "The same kids who were at Sean's party, well, we're all going up north to spend the day at this ski lodge. We're going by car – two cars." I was careful how I put this. I didn't actually want to lie any more than necessary. "Older people will be driving us so it won't cost anything for transportation." I didn't mention, of course, that we might have to go by train, or that older meant seventeen.

"Just a minute, Annie. You said you were going to spend the day at some ski lodge?"

"Not *some* ski lodge. It belongs to Josh Morgenstern's parents. It has a big fireplace and, you know, all the stuff you need."

She was looking at me like I'd just told her I was stowing away on a rocket to the moon.

"Whereabouts is it?"

It dawned on me Sean had never actually mentioned the name of the place. "Oh," I said, offhandedly, "it's one of the small cities. Mountainside or Mountainview, I forget exactly which."

"You mean you're going to travel to somewhere – not even knowing where – with some older kids driving, who've probably been drinking all New Year's Eve and have had no sleep? To freeze in the bitter cold and snow with no decent boots and in *your* jacket. No!"

"No?" My heart was in my ears, and the adrenalin had started to flow. "Mom, why not? These kids will not be up all night drinking. And I'm not going to be outdoors. There's not enough snow up there to ski, even if I could. You don't understand. We're going to be indoors where it'll be warm and cosy, in front of this enormous fireplace. We'll probably roast marshmallows and potatoes and sing songs. It'll be like indoor camping."

For a minute I thought I'd made a point. My mother

looked very pensive. I was certain she was thinking it over and this wasn't the time to force anything. I waited.

"I'll give you some extra money so you can go to a movie tomorrow," she said.

She'd pushed the subject right out of the way, like the breakfast dishes. "When are you going to stop treating me like a baby?" I yelled.

My mother kept deliberately calm. "What are you shouting about, Annie? You come up with a crazy idea and you expect me to agree?"

"If it's not crazy for the other kids why is it crazy for me?"

"We don't use that logic in this house. We never have and we never will." She was walking toward the door.

I called out after her. "What if I went anyway? You couldn't stop me!" In my entire life I'd never thrown that kind of a threat at my mother before. She turned, her face white.

"No, Annabelle, I guess I wouldn't even know how to stop you. But if you're going to do drastic things, save them for something important."

"How would you know what's important to a fourteen-year-old girl? You're always bragging about how you never had a childhood because your parents died when you were so young."

She just shook her head. I couldn't tell if it was because she was disgusted or to let me know she wasn't going to continue with this.

"I know why you treat me like a baby. You're afraid to let me grow up because you know I'll … I'll … go right out and look for my father. And you're right! That's exactly what I'm going to do!"

I went into my room and slammed the door. How did this happen? I hadn't even been thinking of my father. At least, well, maybe. I thought she would just leave the house, but she was right on my heels, opening the door a second after I'd banged it shut.

"Annie," she said, "if I leave with this up in the air we'll both have a miserable day. All I ask is for you to think over calmly how rational your request to go on this trip is. I apologize for being abrupt just now, but I do have to leave for work."

"Then go!" I said, nastily.

I plunked myself down on the bed. My mother was gazing past me with such a wary expression, I turned my head to look.

"Annie, is that money on your bed?"

She sounded just like she looked. I swallowed hard. "Oh, yeah, that."

"Are you ... holding it for someone?"

"No, it's mine." I let out a little self-conscious laugh.

"Yours?" She came over to the bed and spread the bills out. "There's close to a hundred dollars here." She looked at me, completely bewildered.

"Yeah, well, it's part of a surprise. I just hadn't gotten around to telling you yet. What with Christmas and all."

"You didn't mention anything. Baby-sitting?" She smiled at me, but it was a vague, bordering-on-suspicious kind of a smile.

"I really don't want you taking any kind of a job, Annie, without your letting me know the details, even

to surprise me. But I can't believe all this money – "
She made a helpless gesture with her hands.

"Mom, I would never baby-sit any place you didn't
know about. No, you'll never believe how I got it." I
tried to sound mysterious.

"Yes, I'm anxious to hear," she said, leaning against
the bed.

"You mean now?" I asked, surprised. "I thought you
were in a hurry to go to work."

"I can be late."

I took one deep breath. "Well, Mrs. Maxstead – you
know, Bernice's mother? She bought this jacket for her
niece Candy. I told you about her – the girl who died.
So after what happened – she gave it to me."

"What jacket? What are you talking about?"

"Mom, I didn't keep it. I took it back to the store and
got a refund."

My mother sank down on the bed across from me.
"A refund. Why didn't I get to see this jacket?"

"I was afraid you might want me to keep it, you know,
on account of mine being so thin and all. And I didn't
want to keep it, because it was, well, nothing like anyone wears. It was very pretty in a sort of all-dressed-up
party way. I'd stick out in it like a neon sign."

"Why didn't you return it to Mrs. Maxstead?" My
mother's voice got really soft, the way it always did when
she became very serious over something. "She might
have wanted to give it to someone else."

"She was so upset, almost hysterical over it. See, it
reminded her of Candy, and she said to get it out of
her sight and she didn't care what I did with it. Those

were her exact words." I wasn't very convincing, what did the words matter? Meanwhile the money lay there.

"Annie, there's something about this story that doesn't seem right."

"It's not a story!"

"Calm down. I'm only trying to get to the bottom of this."

"What bottom? There is no bottom. It's exactly what I'm telling you!"

"Annie, where did the money for the opera tickets come from?"

I hesitated.

"It was part of this refund, wasn't it?"

"So what? I wanted it to be a surprise."

My mother sat stiffly on the bed. "Annie, you're telling me the store gave you a refund. Without a sales receipt? What store was it?"

I looked over at the money strewn out on the bed – it made me feel nauseous. "Mom, you're missing the point. Which store has nothing to do with it. The important thing is, I intended calling Mrs. Maxstead and tell her I couldn't wear the jacket. But I was being sensitive to her feelings, with the funeral and all. Now I'm being treated like a criminal for being considerate."

"I asked you what store, Annabelle."

"Mannerheim's."

"Mannerheim's," she repeated, making it sound like a national shrine or something. "Mannerheim's, of all stores, doesn't blithely take back merchandise. And I'm equally certain Mrs. Maxstead didn't give you the receipt. So exactly what happened?"

"Are you accusing me of stealing?" I asked harshly.

"No need to raise your voice. I'm attempting to get some answers. Not to accuse you of anything. Now, Annie, how did you get the receipt?"

"Mrs. Maxstead gave me the box – with everything inside."

"So you found it in the box."

"Yes. So she did give it to me, in a way." A look of doom covered my mother's face.

"Mom, you don't understand. Just because we can't afford to be generous and give things away, rich people can. Easily. It's no big deal to them."

"Don't tell me what I can and can't understand. But I'll tell you one thing I certainly can't understand, Annie. What on earth could you have been thinking?"

"If someone gives you something – a gift – anything, well, doesn't it become yours?"

"Annie – " my mother began.

"No," I insisted, "now you answer *me*. Isn't it yours?"

"Well, yes – "

"And what's yours is yours to do with exactly as you please. The jacket didn't suit me, so I returned it for the refund. You're acting as if I stole the Maxsteads' grocery money."

"Annie!"

"Honestly, Mom, you're making too much of this. I know about rich people. I'm with them every day at school. Money like this is chicken-feed to them."

"You seem to have forgotten that I also have some experience with rich people, Annabelle."

I winced.

"What the Maxsteads have or own is not our business," she went on. "I'm not interested in their money."

Suddenly I was really angry. "You're never interested in money. You weren't interested in my father's money, either. That's how I ended up not having money or a father."

There was a long pause. Then my mother said, wearily, "So at last we get to the bottom of it. It all comes down to the Whittledges."

"Here, take the rotten old money," I said, shoving it over roughly with my hands. "I can't even go where I want with my friends." Tears of hurt and anger were swimming in my eyes.

She just sat there.

"What are you going to do?" I asked. Not that I cared anymore.

"I'm not going to do anything. It's what you're going to do, Annie. And that's to think long and hard about what you did."

"How about what bitchy Mrs. Maxstead did? How do you know she didn't trap me deliberately?"

"No, Annie, you trapped yourself. She acted badly, too, I'll grant you, but she's not our problem. Besides, no one forced you to behave as you did. No one twisted your arm, Annie. You did it to yourself. Now I want you to think about *why* you did it."

"I don't have to think," I answered challengingly. "I did it because I want to be like the other kids at school, and that means having money."

"But you don't have money."

"Tell me about it."

"Those girls won't care or notice unless you call attention to it."

"Oh, sure. They notice plenty. They talk and gossip about everything."

"If it bothers you that much, leave the school."

"What?" I couldn't believe she'd actually said that.

"Look, Annie, you have to make a choice. Either you accept the situation as it exists and deal with it or transfer to public school – or evade and lie and cover up every hour of every day. It's hard work, Annie. So decide."

I really wanted to hang tough – to say I didn't care how hard it would be. If the other kids thought I was just like them it would be worth it. Only I couldn't. Instead I broke down crying and slobbering like an idiot. My mother pulled me into her arms. "I'm a first-class sleeze," I sobbed.

"Come on, Annie, that's one thing you're not." She laughed.

I tried to laugh in mid-sob, but it just gave me the hiccups.

"I have to go now. But Annie, think seriously. Then we'll talk it all over." She paused. "Will you be okay?"

I nodded. "You're going to be awfully late for work."

"Yes, but this was more important."

As she got up I saw her eyes dart to and then away from the money. After she left I stared at it, too. It was like I'd never seen it before. Like it was money from some foreign country.

CHAPTER SEVEN

"Everything's set for the lodge, Annie. And we're in luck. We'll be going by car."

I was silent for a moment. "Sean, I can't go."

Now the silence was on his end of the line. "You can't? How come?"

I didn't get any pleasure from hearing the disappointment in his voice this time. "Some other stuff I promised to do before this came up," I lied. "I, uh, I forgot about it."

"Can't you get out of it?"

"Well, no, not really. I'm terribly sorry." The understatement of all time. "I would have let you know sooner, but I knew you were out of town."

"Gee, Annie, I feel awful about this."

"Me, too. I bet it'll be great."

"Not as great as if you were there," he said.

There was nothing more to say, so what was the point? "Well, goodbye, Sean." I hung up.

The rest of the day I felt kind of dead inside.

Then my mother amazed me – again. She splurged for dinner. Instead of making dinner, she brought in Chinese food.

"Hey, Mom, you have to eat it out of the cartons. That makes it authentic."

"Uh-uh," she said, "carton repeats on me," dishing it out on plates.

I was feeling better – at least a little. If the business of the jacket and the money hadn't exploded in my face I'd probably still be sulking in my room, furious with my mother over the trip to the lodge. Only it's hard to be a martyr and a criminal at the same time.

When Joe came by to get my mother I hardly recognized him: grey suit, white shirt and a tie with a small red print. I'd only seen him in jeans or slacks.

"Took your breath away, huh, Annie?" he joked, as I stared at him.

"You look … very nice, Joe."

"Thank you, Annie. I suppose this will be my new working uniform. Did Betts tell you I'm starting a new job in a couple of weeks?"

"Yeah, she did. Congratulations. Go for it."

"Thanks." And then, "Oh, Betts!" as my mother came toward us.

She looked beautiful – kind of sexy, too, which is not one of the ways I think of her. She's bustier than I am –

at least so far – and has great legs.

My mother started to say, "Joe, you look – "

"We're terrific," he cut in, going around the sofa to kiss her.

I asked her if I could call Linda in Bakersville and wish her a Happy New Year.

"All right, Annie, only don't stay talking forever."

Joe kissed me and wished me a Happy New Year as they were about to leave. Now, if I had waited till now to ask my mother about going to the lodge she might just have said yes. And the whole thing with the jacket never would have happened. And then – but by now Sean would have asked someone else.

I called Linda, who whooped with delight at hearing my voice.

"So," she said, "my New Year's Eve date. May I have this dance?"

"Sure, but you're the one with the boyfriend."

"A lot of good it does me. He's not allowed to go out on New Year's Eve, and neither am I. Gets too wild up here in the centre of the universe."

"Boy, what a bunch of fluff toughs you are. Or was it tough fluffs?"

"Tough luck's what it is. Oh, well, how's the rich boy?"

"Busy spending his money." I told her about the trip.

"That's a bummer. But I warned you, Annie – four bathrooms – uh, uh."

"Yeah, you may be right."

After we hung up I was sorry the TV hadn't been fixed. I wasn't in the mood for reading, and there was bound to be a movie or something. Instead, I finished up the cards to my public-school friends. I'd mail them tomorrow. Nice way to start the New Year.

The next morning I was surprised to find my mother up when I headed for the kitchen. "Mom, I thought you'd still be sleeping. Did you get home very late?"

"Not really. Joe's cousin's party had so many people jammed into the house, you couldn't find any place to put yourself." She laughed lightly. "We left after a little while and drove down to Little Italy to a neighbourhood bar. But it was mobbed, too."

There was a long moment of silence.

"Annie, Joe and I had a very serious discussion last night."

My heart sank. "Oh?"

"Of course it wasn't the first, except this time we reached a decision."

My stomach churned.

"I guess we realized we'd come to the point of no return. About marriage."

"What did you tell him?" I asked apprehensively.

"That I was scared. That I had never been married. That it was going to mean a big change, just when I was getting on my feet. Then I told him it was going to be an equally big change for you. That I was the only person you had ever lived with. And being a teenager was traumatic enough."

I shrugged.

"Joe said he was scared, too. That he had already failed at marriage once. But that he loved me and believed he could be a good father to you."

The one word I didn't want to hear. I watched my mother preparing breakfast like nothing unusual was swooping around in our lives.

"You know something, Annie, you and I have always taken chances. From the very start when I decided not to have the abortion the Whittledges wanted me to."

"The Whittledges wanted you to kill me?"

"Annie! What a thing to say!"

"Mom, I never knew you were against abortion."

"I'm not. I wasn't back then, either."

"What changed your mind?" I reached over and touched her hand. "Whatever it was, I'm glad."

She smiled at me.

"Everyone tried talking me out of it. Their arguments were all very sensible – what a struggle it would be having a child in my circumstances, and all that." She paused. "But, Annie, my friends all had families. I had no one. Except the family that was growing inside of me. To have destroyed that – you – would have been like pulling out my own heart."

She pushed the food around her plate. All the times she'd said to me, "Annie, your father didn't want us," I hadn't believed it. Finally I knew what she meant.

"Mom," I said, quietly. "I thought he loved you."

My mother sighed. "Ben was very immature, Annie. Maybe I didn't realize it then because he was so brilliant, but he was afraid of his parents. They were very controlling. If they could have put a ring in his nose and led him around, they would have."

Mrs. Maxstead and Bernice.

"Mrs. Whittledge never forgave me because Ben left

Yale to attend my college. And when I refused to have an abortion they threatened me. They said they could have the baby taken away. I got frightening letters from lawyers. Powerful people don't like to be crossed.

"I think Ben did love me, but he was terrified. At the very beginning he tried to stand by me emotionally. I think he admired my gumption. But when his parents decided to ship him off to Europe, he didn't resist.

"By then I was so weary of the Whittledges that I was more than ready to sign all the papers their lawyers had drawn up – absolving Ben of any obligations. Shortly after that I left school and came to the city to get on with my life."

She studied my face for a long time.

"So, Annie, I'm ready now to take a chance on a husband ... Do you think you could take a chance on a father? A *real* father. I've watched Joe pretty closely when he's with Mathew. It's his nature to be fair and decent. Besides – " she smiled wistfully " – I know something about fathers. I had such a good one. I feel like I'm able to give you a long-overdue gift." She looked ready to laugh and cry at the same time. "Hey, I can give great advice about fathers. But you can't tell me one single thing about husbands."

"You and Joe decided, didn't you."

"Yes. March the first."

My heart wasn't thumping. I still was scared, but you always get scared when you take a chance on something. The phone rang.

"No," I heard her say, "I've been up for quite a while. Annie and I have been having a heart to heart. Sounds great. We'll be ready." She hung up and came back to the table. "Joe's going to get Mathew and we're going out for brunch to celebrate, okay?"

"Fine. Lucky we didn't eat breakfast." We both laughed long and hard, and together.

I went to get ready and glanced out the window on my way. It looked like it might snow. I wondered if the weather would be the same up north. They'd be on their way by now. I was still disappointed I wasn't going, but not angry anymore. I had this feeling – I just knew Sean was going to ask me to go someplace with him again. Unless I asked him first. We could go to an exhibit at one of the museums. Or to see a play at a community house or library. He probably doesn't even know about stuff that's free. I might even bring him down to Tenth Street. I could feel a laugh starting down inside of me. Except ... what about the bathrooms? What did I have in common with four bathrooms?